VACA~~TION~~

Princess of Hell, #4

Eve Langlais

COPYRIGHT & DISCLAIMER

Copyright © October 2015, Eve Langlais
Cover Art by Amanda Kelsey RazzDazz Design © September 2015
Edited by Devin Govaere
Copy Edited by Mandy Pederick
Line Edited by Brieanna Roberston
Produced in Canada

Published by Eve Langlais
1606 Main Street, PO Box 151
Stittsville, Ontario, Canada, K2S1A3
http://www.EveLanglais.com

ISBN-13: 978-1518890666
ISBN-10: 1518890660

CHAPTER ONE

Blinking didn't erase the horror. The permanent marker squiggle went from the front door, along the hallway wall in a determined straight line, rounded over the console table that held the bowl for our keys, down a doorjamb, across the white tile floor then back up the wall. This impressively long piece of art ran the whole length of the corridor on the main floor and right into the living room, where I found the culprit lying on the once pristine white shag rug, once being the key word. Now, my beautiful fluffy treat, which I'd paid an exorbitant sum for, sported hand-drawn zebra stripes. Sob.

In an age-old posture adopted by many a parent, I planted my hands on my hips and, in my sternest voice, said, "What did you do?" In the pit, imps would have trembled, the damned would have thrown themselves prostrate on the floor. Not my daughter, though.

The biggest eyes, graced with thick lashes, set in a face highlighted by chubby cheeks and framed by golden hair pinned in pigtails peeked at me. "Hi, Mommy. Do you like my drawing?"

Must. Resist. The cuteness.

I held firm. No wavering. "Baby girl, you cannot write on the walls."

"Why?"

A word I truly had begun to hate. "Because I just had them painted."

"But they're boring. I made them pretty." She blinked her ridiculously thick and natural eyelashes at me to no avail. I had been raised in the pit. Her guileless expression did not fool me.

"The walls are supposed to be boring, and marker free." After the chaos of Hell, and even everyday life, I enjoyed a home with a simple color palette. Lots of whites and grays, as well as soft blues. No reds or browns or that weird in-between umber here.

"Can I draw on the ceiling then? Poppa's palace has pictures on his."

Poppa's palace had many things

etched into his ceiling, some of them quite inappropriate for little girls' eyes—and even adult ones, too.

"No." I didn't ask or leave any wiggle room. As boss in this relationship, I called the shots.

"Why?"

Argh, there was that damned word again. Time to foil her with logic. "Because you're supposed to write on paper."

"But Poppa says only fools and goody-two-shoes do what they're supposed to. The"—she wrinkled her snub nose adorably—"intrepid forge their own rules." She beamed, and I saw the slyness in her expression.

I blinked. How could I argue when I'd been raised on the same rule? That was what happened when you had the devil for your daughter's grandfather. He filled her head with the same nonsense as he'd filled mine. And I turned out great, but still, even as a child, I learned that parents must be obeyed—or I lost special privileges like chocolate pudding for dessert and I got medical journals for my birthday instead of pretty shiny things.

Lucinda, the ruby-red apple of my eye, had not yet grasped the knowledge that I was in charge. Never mind the fact I still didn't listen to my father. I would do better than him. I would set rules and boundaries and expect them to be obeyed.

"I will not have you turn our home into a graffiti studio. No more drawing on anything but paper. Is that understood?" I threw in a proper mommy glare for good measure.

Her lips turned down. Trembled. "Don't be mad, Mommy. I love you." She then unleashed her weapon of parental destruction. The dimple. It was deep, adorable, and matched with twinkling eyes.

But the thing with being related to the devil was you recognized manipulation when it happened. Unlike Lucinda's fathers, I didn't fall for it. "Go to your room." Head tilted imperially, I pointed to the door.

Lip jutting in a powerful sulk, Lucinda rose to her feet. My baby girl was growing so fast. Only a few months old, and yet already she looked like a child much older, four or five at least, with a vocabulary to put even most adults to shame. Then again, she hadn't had a classic entrance to the world or upbringing.

She'd also decided to test my last nerve by dragging her uncapped marker across the white leather armrest of the couch as she walked by.

Oh hell no. "Get to your room!" I yelled. "Right now, missy. No television. No video games. And no ice cream for dessert either."

"You suck!" she hollered back.

I did, but only my special harem of men. But that wasn't the point right now. "You're also grounded," I added to her retreating back. "And don't you come out of that room until you're ready to scrub the mess you made and apologize."

She growled, but caused no further destruction on her path. Phew. And dammit! She was right. I did suck at this whole parenting thing.

According to the book I got on raising kids, tip one of being a good parent was 'Never yell'. I failed that within the first week of living with my daughter. In my defense, this whole motherhood thing was kind of a shock.

For those not familiar with my past, it wasn't that long ago I found out I was pregnant by two men. Yes, I am that kind of girl, and yes, I am still with both of them, with an added third, but he wasn't present at the time of my world-changing conception.

Not long after the discovery of my shocking pregnancy, I was kidnapped and taken to an alternate dimension, drugged, and kept prisoner, for what seemed like weeks and months but was, in actuality, only days in the real world. But there was a reason for this accelerated time pocket.

As soon as my baby proved viable, Lilith and her goons literally ripped Lucinda from my body and left me for dead. I would have died that day except my mother, much as I hated to give her any credit, came to my rescue and saved me. Healed me, too.

Dear old mom then kidnapped my newborn daughter, and that was when I kind of lost my shit. In her defense, my mother thought she was protecting the world from a horrible fate. AKA my daughter. Apparently, my baby girl had the power to possibly destroy the world.

I didn't care.

My daughter might be the equivalent of a nuclear bomb in a pink romper with pigtails and the cutest little sandals—so cute I bought them in four colors—but she was mine. All mine. And, boy, was she proving to be a handful.

My father called it payback for the hell I'd put him through. Disliking his chuckling reply to my woes, I threw cement in his favorite horned duckie boots. Revenge was a specialty of mine.

Real life, family life, was a lot harder than they portrayed on television. Juggling a happily-ever-after with a fallen angel who was my soulmate took compromises on my part. The good habits Auric had accrued over the years took some work to corrupt.

As if one consort with altruistic goals wasn't enough, along slinked a hunky cat shifter who stole my heart and did wicked things with that rough tongue of his. David took pussy licking to a whole new level.

Two lovers should have been enough, but I was cursed with a nymphotype of magic that needed, make that craved, sex and arousal. My greedy power attracted yet a third man to my ménage, a dark and sexy vampire.

Some might say I should have resisted. Yeah. Okay. They'd obviously not met Teivel. Imagine if you would that last piece of forbidden chocolate, the creamy, melt-in-your-mouth decadence that you should deny. But couldn't. It didn't help that, at the time, I needed him in a sexual menagerie to unlock a new aspect of my magic so I could save my daughter.

The fact that the sex was out of this world didn't play a part in me keeping him. Much.

Despite a part of me screaming that having three lovers was wrong, I couldn't just dump Teivel—and not just because he'd share his blood with me. A connection beyond the physical existed between me and all of my men, and I'd found a precariously balanced happiness, one that took careful attention.

Add in a precocious little girl, who was spoiled rotten and thought the world revolved around her—which it did on more than one occasion because of my blasted mother who enjoyed playing the part of doting nana—and my life was a never-ending series of dramas, foot stomping, yelling, and tears. By me.

No one had ever explained that being a grownup meant so much damned work—and paint and Lysol wipes and Tide-to-Go sticks—which was why I decided we needed a vacation. More accurately, I needed one, but apparently, I couldn't just pack a bag, hoist it over a shoulder, and jump on the first flight to the Caribbean. Or so Auric informed me with his arms crossed over his chest as he glared at me from the doorway I'd planned to sneak out of.

"And just where do you think you're going?" he asked in that deep growl of his that never failed to get my nerves tingling.

"Hey, stud muffin. You're looking awfully sexy today. Wanna go for a quickie?" One for the road, so to speak.

"Yes, but only after you explain the bag from which I see dangling a bikini string."

Quick, I needed a believable lie. As

Lucifer's daughter, it was expected of me. "I'm going tanning." If this were the *Family Feud*, I would have totally scored big points on that answer, but just in case, for good measure, I batted my lashes innocently. It usually worked on David.

Auric wasn't David and he didn't fall for it. Jerk.

He asked again. "What harebrained scheme are you planning now?" He leaned against the doorjamb, blocking my path, his arms crossed over his wide chest.

Time for lie number two. "The gym?" That sounded plausible, right?

Giant X with a great big buzzer sound.

A snort escaped him. "The gym? You hate regimented exercise. You're always complaining to your dad about the evilness of the trainers who want to put your body through rigorous training."

I'd said that? Probably. Funny how weapons training and a jog—sometimes chasing wannabe muggers—was filed under fun in my books, but physical fitness with the pure intent of toning muscle drove me up the wall. "Well, maybe I changed my mind."

"Says the liar wearing shades, a floppy straw hat, and a sarong cover-up over yet another skimpy bikini. I know you're still trying to impress your dad with your lying abilities—"

"Am not," I protested.

"But as my life partner and mother of our child, you cannot just slip away without letting people know where you're going."

"Why not?" I pouted.

"Because there are people who care for you and might get worried."

"I have a cell phone." Packed somewhere. I thought. I'd kind of rushed in an attempt to avoid my significant other with all his questions.

"Are you sure?"

David's purred words right next to my ear made me squeak and jump. Damned cat was always sneaking up on me. I really needed to put a bell on him.

"I'm pretty sure I grabbed it." Yet another lie shot down as a smartphone, encased in a pink cover with glittery diamonds, was waved in front of my face.

"Are you sure it's mine?" I said weakly.

"I am pretty sure it's not mine," David replied.

Auric just shook his head and sighed.

"Oops. Did I forget it again?" A feigned giggle that didn't do a thing to wipe Auric's expression.

"Muriel, baby, I realize you're feeling a little stressed right now with all the responsibilities—"

"No, I'm not." A whopper of a fib that probably earned me a gold star in Dad's books.

A snicker from behind me as David murmured. "Keep digging. I don't think that hole is big enough."

And apparently neither was that shoe because every time I opened my mouth, I made it worse. "I'm fine. Really. I was just, um, ugh." Even I couldn't keep the stream of untruths coming. "Fine. I'm feeling a little stressed and super overwhelmed. I suck at the mommy thing." I dumped my hastily packed bag on the floor and kicked it.

"You do not, and it's normal to feel that way," Auric replied. His tone was meant to be soothing, yet I didn't feel it.

"No, it's not normal. I mean people become mothers every day. And I didn't even have to go through the whole diaper part. I have no reason to be stressed. She's bright and beautiful and…"

"Willful," Auric added.

"Precocious," was David's addition.

She was also much too smart for her age. The experiences she'd had when running from Lilith, and, yes, I meant the original Lilith cast from the garden and bent on revenge, meant Lucinda was different from other children.

"So my kid is just like me. Great. I am so screwed." I flopped onto my bag and stuck my head between my knees.

A broad hand rubbed my back as Auric knelt beside me. "Yes, she is a lot like you—perfect, but at the same time, tiring."

"Hey, are you calling me a PITA?" For the uninformed, that was the polite way of saying pain in the ass.

"I love how you are, who you are, but at times, I'll admit, I'm glad I've got backup." Backup being David and Teivel and… No one. Hello, there was no other.

Yet. The threat just kind of floated in my mind.

I shivered. Was it me or did a breeze just coast through the hall, bringing with it the briny scent of the ocean? I'd been having lots of incidences like that recently. Urges to submerse myself in water. Odd whiffs of ocean matter like seawater and seaweed and even that ugh smell from something dead washed upon the shore.

Either we had a weird problem in our house or something strange was afoot—or should I say afloat?

Fingers snapped in front of my face, forcing me to focus on the here and now, which included an irritated-looking Auric. "You aren't listening."

This time I didn't bother to lie. "Nope. I need to go to the ocean." The words left my mouth without warning. But once said, I could feel the truth of them. Something called me. Something wanted me to go to the beach.

Connected to me on an emotionally deep level, Auric caught some of what I felt. Or, at least, focused in on a certain choice of words. "Need?"

I nodded.

David frowned while Auric bore a thoughtful expression. "I thought you hated the beach because the sand gets in your unmentionables and you scream like a little girl when slimy things like fish or seaweed touch you."

"I do hate those things." Especially the sand-in-the-crotch. I swear I rinsed the stuff off me for weeks after the few times Daddy dragged me on a vacation in Hell. Literally. We used to take our summer holidays by the Darkling Sea in a villa he owned set high on the bluffs.

I grew to hate those forced family excursions, to the amusement of my sister, Bambi, who totally rocked a bikini and could eat sushi with a groan of pleasure.

Put raw seafood near my lips and I didn't just gag. I hugged the porcelain of the nearest toilet. So my sudden fetish for the ocean wasn't just unexpected, it was—

"Unnatural." Auric stroked his chin. "So why are you suddenly so eager to go to the one place you dislike?"

"I don't dislike the ocean and beach,"

I protested, "so long as I'm inside a resort, looking at it through a window while getting a massage and being hand-fed chocolate-covered strawberries."

"That kind of defeats the purpose of going somewhere tropical," Auric pointed out.

Him and his logic. I'd fight it with irrationality. "Not really because that's where you get the best drinks with those cute little cocktail umbrellas."

"I know, how about instead of visiting the ocean, which you hate, we have a family vacation in Canada? We could drive through the Rockies. Commune with nature."

That sounded fun actually. The last time I'd gone, I had a fabulous time hanging with the Sasquatch. Those big, hairy dudes could party. I also quite enjoyed outdoor lovemaking. Ooh, and hot-tubbing outdoors at night while listening the wildlife.

It sounded great. Fun. Just what I needed, which was why I said, "No. I need to go to the beach."

I slapped a hand over my mouth, and

that might have been why Auric's gaze narrowed. His tone very careful, he said, "What about Disneyland? Lucinda would love it, and you could both dress as princesses and scream 'off with their heads!' until they escort you out."

Hell yeah. I'd had such fun that day Auric had taken me. We'd no sooner made it off the hallowed Disney grounds than he took me, fluffy skirts up over my head. Good times, and something I wouldn't mind doing again. So I said, "No. I *need* to go to the beach."

There was something utterly annoying about two men exchanging significant glances. I totally hated it. Yet it happened often around me, especially when weird stuff happened, like my head thinking one thing and my mouth saying another.

"Muriel, why don't you head upstairs and have a nice, long bath. David and I will keep an eye on Lucinda and figure out something we can do for a family vacation."

Sounded great. Me, a deep tub, and bubbles that tickled my nose.

I might have blinked as I walked into David's chest, which happened to be standing in front of the door. "Tub's upstairs," he reminded.

A high-pitched titter left me. "Oops. Wrong way." Yet what truly felt like the wrong way was my feet going up the steps instead of out the door. Auric was right. There was something seriously wrong with me.

And I wasn't just talking about my mental state. That was hereditary.

CHAPTER TWO

The swish of her ass in that translucent sarong proved enticing, especially since her bikini bottom barely covered her full, heart-shaped ass. Yet Auric didn't chase after her. Other things required his attention.

Muriel had no sooner disappeared out of sight when Auric turned to David. "I think we have a problem."

"You think? I'd heard of postpartum depression, but this is crazy," David said.

Auric's shaggy-blond-haired friend still stared at the top of the stairs, even though Muriel was out of sight.

Did he fear she'd come flying down, determined to exit that front door again? He wasn't alone.

"I think what we just saw was more than a case of her adjusting to being a mother and home life."

The comment drew David's glance. "You think someone's cast a spell on her?"

Auric lifted his shoulders. "Maybe, and yet, at the same time, I don't get the same feeling as the last time she had that problem." The last time being when they'd been dealing with Gabriel and a spell of fear he'd placed on Muriel's mind. "This seems like more of a compulsion."

"Or a craving, like pregnant women get for pickles and peanut butter."

Could she be pregnant? The old crone who examined her after everything calmed down claimed Muriel would never have another child. Even though she'd healed, the damage done when Lucinda was taken from her body had destroyed that chance.

I don't think it's hormones, though. Something else was at work, and he didn't like it one bit.

I need to call a meeting. The sooner the better.

Auric moved away from the front door, paused, and pivoted back. He tapped at the keypad and armed the house alarm. Then he traced a symbol on the wall, activating the magical wards on the house.

"Are you worried someone might be

trying to get in? Usually that's not a problem in the daytime." As David moved from the wall, his casual slouch morphed into a more alert position. The predator in him came alive.

Jaw set, Auric revealed, "It's not something getting in that worries me. We could all use a bit of exercise. I'm more concerned that a certain someone will attempt to get out."

For those who wondered, the wards would stop even Muriel from opening a portal to escape. The protective web on the house had been put in place by Nefertiti herself, one of the strongest sorceresses ever. Once Auric activated them, he could rest assured that Muriel couldn't bypass it.

Yet.

As the old sorceress had warned Auric, "Her magic is growing. What she can't do today might not apply to tomorrow." Not reassuring, but then again, he'd not fallen in love with Muriel because she was normal and safe.

"Do you think she'll really try and escape so she can go to the beach?" David asked as he matched Auric's pace down the hall, a hall he noted sported a new dark line. *I see my daughter's been expressing her artistic side again.*

No wonder Muriel was in a tizzy. For a girl raised by the devil, she had certain notions when it came to behavior. She might not enforce the traditional please and thank-yous, but she did expect respect and had become OCD as of late about their home. A tidy Muriel was scarier than the slob he'd first met.

In reply to David's query, he said, "Am I worried she'll escape? Fucking right I am. This is Muriel we're talking about." And that said it all.

Headstrong, single-minded, and fearless, Muriel would not hesitate to charge into the fray with no thought beyond doing her version of the right thing. It was one of her most frustrating and endearing qualities.

She keeps life from growing stale.

A man never knew what she'd do next. What madness she'd wreak. What chaos she'd provoke.

Armed with this expectation, Auric could admit he needed reinforcements. He already had a certain cat on board. Time to recruit some others.

The gleaming kitchen, with its superbly modern cupboards in white, showed fingerprints, tiny ones in a variety of flavors.

Chocolate. Muriel's fave. Peanut butter, smeared on the white subway tile backsplash, was something David ate by the spoonful. The bottle tipped over on the table was root beer, Lucinda's flavor choice. Auric usually preferred his without the root.

It seemed a certain sticky-fingered girl took after her parents. And certainly put her mark on things.

David took a peek and whistled. "No wonder Muriel is losing her shit today. This is bad."

"Bad? It's a kid being a kid." Auric saw the mess and thought not much of it. Kids were messy.

Except David didn't agree. "This is doing it on purpose. The kitchen was spotless this morning, and Lucinda is a smart kid. There is no way a single child, in that span of time, could naturally cause such a mess. This took someone with special skills."

No use in getting offended over the fact that David had called their child different. Couldn't argue the truth. "But why?" Why purposely drive her mother to mental exhaustion?

The idea niggled as they bypassed the opening leading to the mudroom, which had gone from bleached haven to…

"Did a squirrel get loose in there?" What else could explain the mud marks on the ceiling? And yet another clue to Muriel's exhausted state.

The next door was closed, and Auric yanked it open. No disaster here, just an ominous pathway down into the bowels of the house. He entered the basement with David on his heels. The door, on a pneumatic hinge, swung shut behind him, but LED lights inset on the steps illuminated the path downward leading to the vampire's lair, Teivel's home in the daytime. While the soulless bastard was tough, he truly couldn't handle sunlight.

As Auric tread down the stairs, it hit him how far he'd come since he'd met

Muriel months ago.

He'd begun life as an angel, and he meant literally began. People had often mused upon where angels came from. He could answer with absolute certainty…that no one knew. Or, if they did, they kept it a secret.

All Auric remembered of his awakening was opening his eyes and a feminine voice saying, *"Welcome to heaven. Please put on this robe."* Strange, and yet everyone he dared ask that was angelic in nature repeated the same experience. His kind couldn't procreate with themselves, only humans and certain types of demons. As a mixture of both, Muriel proved capable also of bearing him a child. Even if she couldn't, he would have fallen for her anyway.

Muriel presented the ultimate forbidden fruit, and once he'd found himself enthralled by her, he finally understood why Adam and Eve had disobeyed.

He should note, though, that she wasn't the reason for his fall or disgrace. His disobedience began before he'd even met Muriel. Originally, Auric served as a soldier in God's Army of Light. Endless days of pretty sword work and flight drills. Only rarely were the soldiers of Heaven called into action.

But the thing was, once Auric tasted the allure of battle in fighting for justice and peace...that was where he perhaps committed his first sin. The sin of enjoyment.

He enjoyed helping others. He wanted to do more, so he asked his superiors what else they could do to help mankind.

Nothing was their answer. Those in charge let the injustices of the world continue. They refused to act. Auric didn't understand. Did they not want man to ascend to Heaven?

At the time, he still held unwavering belief, a belief that faltered as tragedies continued to occur. He watched as atrocities unfolded that would have enjoyed a different outcome if only the angels intervened. It frustrated him to sit and do nothing. A champion was needed. His sword could make a difference, so

Auric demanded they help the mortals fighting the day-to-day battles against sins and other Hellish conflicts.

He was forbidden, and they tired of him questioning.

He tired of them not acting, so he took matters into his own hands.

For his disobedience, Auric found himself tried, convicted, and cast from Heaven. Thrown down upon the earth to live among the mortals, without his wings, without any magic, just a man looking to make a difference.

It didn't take long to realize that one sword could only wreak so much justice. He needed allies and found them. Along his quest to rid the world of evil, he discovered like-minded men. And only men because Auric tended to stay far from women. Raised in a sexist culture—because God truly had defined ideas of the roles of men and women—Auric remained true to his roots until one day a woman slammed into him, a woman whose scent of hot cinnamon and pure lust hit him like a train. He'd walked away from that first encounter stunned by his reaction, only to find Muriel again when he walked into a certain bar.

From that moment on, he was hooked. He stalked her, and not just because Muriel was the daughter of Lucifer, seed of evil. A seed for redemption. Heaven gave him a chance for pardon. He just needed to do one little favor. Kill her.

He'd rather kill himself.

From the moment Auric met Muriel, she became his new reason for being. Yes, she was sinful—especially between the sheets—and yet, at the same time, she had a core of goodness, a need to help others and do the right thing, even if it sometimes drove Lucifer mad.

How he loved that about her. How he loved her. And because of that love, Auric now lived a life he'd never imagined, but only because he'd let his mind open to the fact that not everything that happened was as black and white as the scriptures stated. There definitely existed a gray area, the area most people fell into. An area that suited Auric just fine, as it let him act as he saw fit. Because of this gray spot between extremes, he could have a life with the woman who completed him. The one woman who gave a fallen angel a place to belong, a woman he had to share with two other men.

People might spout sharing is caring. Like fuck. And, yes, he could curse, just like he could covet with the best of them.

What man wanted to turn mine into ours? Certainly not him. He wanted Muriel all for himself. If only her innate magic hadn't made that impossible. But he couldn't fight the truth. Auric alone was not enough to fuel her magic.

No big deal, some would say. How strong a magic did she need? The strongest. Even Auric could state that because he knew Muriel was destined for great things. He'd seen her do the impossible.

Fate kept tossing rocks at her, tough things that required Muriel to hold strong. Strength meant feeding her magic, and thus did his best friend, David, join them. Having sex with Muriel and another guy didn't prove as traumatizing as he'd feared. Actually, another guy in the bedroom amped things to the next level.

With the dual magic she siphoned from their orgasmic pleasure, Muriel had played a large part in saving Hell when it froze.

When they'd defeated Gabriel, they stayed a trio and, not long after, found out about the pregnancy. Not surprising, shit happened again, in the form of Lilith, a first-generation bitch determined to rule Hell, Heaven, the Earth. In other words, anything she could get her greedy hands on.

Lilith was gone, but the magic they required to vanquish her meant they'd acquired another man.

And then we were four.

Actually five with Lucinda now living with them.

One big freaking family and yet, Auric feared it was about to grow.

The living room at the bottom of the basement stairs didn't remain dark long as Auric barked, "Lights." They came on suddenly, but muted, the recessed lighting soft and subtle in this cavern of a place.

There were no windows in the basement. The walls were painted a deep blue, while the furniture sported creamy black leather. One entire wall was comprised by a large screen—with a kick-ass projector providing the best Sunday night football ever.

Welcome to the lair, the ultimate man cave replete with all the game systems, surround sound, and a fully stocked bar.

But today wasn't about hanging out. An emergency strategy session was required, but for that, he needed to call in a few more key players.

Auric yanked out his phone and sent a group message then strode to the only closed door, a leather-studded eight-footer, and banged on it.

David dropped onto the couch and aimed a remote. The screen flickered to life, and a dozen camera boxes appeared, each a different section of the house.

"Do you see her?"

"Yup. She's running the water and dumping tons of shit in it."

"So long as she's here, that's good." *Bang. Bang. Bang.* Auric hammered the portal again and hollered. "Hey, dead dude, get your ass out here. We have a situation."

The ankle sweep proved surprising, yet Auric recovered quickly. He back sprung and landed in a crouch. Arms tucked to his sides, he presented loose fists to Teivel.

A lazy smile stretched the vampire's face. "Your reflexes are getting better, choir boy."

"All the better to fool you with, fang."

Teivel snickered as he took a seat in a club chair. He reclined and drummed long fingers on the armrest. "What's got your blood rushing?"

Having Teivel remark upon his mood based on the flow of his blood was something Auric had grown accustomed to. For a blood-sucking, soulless fiend, Teivel wasn't a bad sort, and when it came to protecting Muriel and Lucinda, he proved a strong ally.

"Muriel's acting weird."

"And this is unusual because?" The arched brow went well with the sarcasm.

"She wants to go to the beach," David supplied.

"I thought she hated it."

"She does," Auric and David replied in unison.

"How badly does she want to go?"

The screen flickered and zoomed to one large image of Muriel dumping a decorative basket of seashells in the water. The goldfish and all his colored stone went in next, as did a certain doll with a shimmery tail.

"What the fuck is she doing?"

"I think she's trying to create a beach," Auric answered.

"Why?"

The half-second whiff of brimstone gave him warning, so he didn't let out an unmanly yell when a smooth, car salesman's voice boomed, "She's trying to recreate warm, fuzzy memories of her childhood. Why, I still so clearly recall her expression every March break when I told her we were going to the beach for a vacation."

"You do know she hated those beach visits."

The wide smile on Lucifer's face stretched wider. "Of course she did. Who wants a perfectly boring, no excitement holiday? I gave her something to remember and talk about."

"Despite your twisted philosophy, I'm pretty sure she doesn't want to go the beach."

"Who doesn't want to go to the beach?" Mother Nature popped in on a springtime breeze of fresh-cut grass.

"Are you stalking me again?" Lucifer turned to glare suspiciously at Gaia.

"It's not stalking if we're dating. It's called an unhealthy suspicion of your activities." Mother Nature wore a smile Auric knew all too well. Now he knew where Muriel got it from.

"I hate it when you twist my own sins against me."

"I know. Which is why you're obsessed with me."

"I am not obsessed."

"Says the man who put cameras in my garden. You bring possessiveness and jealousy to a new level, Luc. And, even better, your perverted attention provides a great example to your minions."

And there was the guileless expression Auric recognized from both

Muriel and Lucinda's faces. Poor Lucifer didn't stand a chance.

"I will not discuss the fact that you exploit my weakness, wench. Grave matters are afoot. I sense a change in the force."

"Would you stop it with the *Star Wars* references already." Gaia rolled her eyes.

Lucifer promptly replied with a short, spittle-laced raspberry. "I meant the force between worlds. Incoming portal." He pointed, and sure enough, a rip opened.

That made three portals in only a few minutes. What the fuck? "Why is the concept of ringing the doorbell so bloody hard?"

"It's a waste of time, and much too polite. I prefer the element of surprise," Lucifer said. "I catch more people sinning that way."

"How did you guys open doorways to here anyhow? I set the wards on the house."

To which both Lucifer and Gaia twittered. "Nefertiti is my witch," Lucifer reminded. "As such, we had a backdoor put in for our use only."

"That doesn't explain how Bambi and Chris got here." He stabbed a finger at Muriel's sister, who strode into view wearing knee-high bitchin' boots, as Muriel would say. Her dress had a skirt that actually fluttered to mid-thigh, and the neckline only plunged halfway. Pretty conservative, considering the outfits she'd donned in the past. Auric wondered if the guy by her side was to blame.

Chris, another good friend, and a wizard who often fought by Auric's side, held up his hands in a gesture of innocence. "Wasn't me. I still can't do portals."

At Auric's glance at Bambi, she also held her hands in surrender, but the sensuality of it still didn't make her look innocent. "I didn't do it either. Lucinda did."

A frown creased his brow. "What do you mean Lucinda did? That's not possible. She's in her room playing dolls."

As if to prove Auric's statement, one of the camera views took over the big screen to show Lucinda in her room, sitting cross-legged on the floor in front of her large dollhouse, a naked doll with shorn hair dancing in front of it.

"She hasn't moved since I flipped the cameras on a few minutes ago."

"That child is incredibly gifted." Said by the proud grandmother.

His sweet daughter was also oddly jointed, given she turned her head a full one hundred and eighty degrees and smiled at the camera.

While other people might freak and call a priest, Auric understood that, no matter what, she was his baby girl and, according to Lucifer, "An apt student. She's obviously been practicing, something I usually hate, as it shows a steadfast determination, but given it's also a sign of her admiration for her grandpa, completely acceptable in this case."

Welcome to Lucifer's world. It was slightly twisted, but not so bad once you got used to it.

With the whole gang gathered, Auric quickly gave them a rundown of what was happening. At the end of it all, Auric wasn't alone in wearing a concerned expression.

Lucifer started the discussion. "Aim me in a direction and I'll kill whatever is fucking with her. I just got my cape back from the cleaners, and my boots are much too clean."

"Can't kill it if we don't know who it is," Chris pointed out, and was it Auric, or was he trying much too hard to avoid looking Bambi's way? And exactly why had the pair of them been together when Lucinda supposedly opened that portal?

"Why must we assume it needs killing?" Bambi's question met shocked silence for a minute then snickers.

"Since when doesn't it require killing?" Lucifer scoffed. "Being old school, I'm more of the torture-them-for-an-eternity sort, but I have to say that Muriel's more efficient method of head lopping does mean less paperwork and, in turn, allows for more golf time."

"You and your golf. You're a man of business," Gaia reminded. "A leader that needs to pay more attention to his kingdom."

"Way to suck the fun away from a

man."

"You're welcome," Gaia sassed.

"You'll pay for those polite manners later," Lucifer threatened.

"I look forward to it. In the meantime, while you two discuss what's up with Muriel's beach obsession, I'm going to play dolls and have a talk with my granddaughter."

With a lingering scent of wild roses, Gaia popped out of the basement, but they all saw her appear on the screen and plop down to the floor, not mindful of her skirts at all.

"That woman is much too sassy," Lucifer grumbled. "Can you believe she's been pressuring me to get married?"

"The horror," Auric retorted dryly. Surely Hell would freeze over again before such a wacky thing happened. "But I'm less concerned about your perverted relationship with Muriel's mom than I am about Muriel herself. Something is wrong with her. I say we take her to Nefertiti. The crone might know what's wrong with her."

"Maybe it's another spell that needs special magic." David couldn't help but grin, especially since every time they needed Muriel magically charged, it meant a mind-blowing orgy.

"Couldn't we just take her to the beach and see what happens?" Bambi suggested.

Possibly put her in harm's way? "Never." Auric never wanted to live through the anguish he'd experienced when he'd thought Muriel was gone forever.

"The succubus has a point," Teivel interjected.

"She has a name," Chris growled.

A sharp clapping of hands showed Lucifer beaming. "Excellent tension and truly magnificent glares, but could we go a little lighter on the whole protecting-her-honor act?"

"It's not an act."

"I know, which is the pity of it," Lucifer complained.

Bambi reached out and put her hand on Chris's arm. Chris didn't physically move, but Auric noted his frame tightened, and was that a tic by his eye? "It's all right. I'm not ashamed of who I am." There was an underlying tone to her words, something that Auric would wager was for Chris alone.

Others, like Teivel, also picked up on it. "Can you two hash out your relationship woes later? We are here for Muriel and her sudden obsession with the ocean. I agree with Bambi's suggestion. Take her to the beach. See what happens."

"You want to put her in harm's way." Flatly stated.

"How is it harmful if we're all there? You're not thinking straight. You said it yourself. She was like a mindless zombie, trying to obey some subliminal order. What if it gets worse? Are you going to follow her every second of every day? Maybe chain her down so she can't leave?"

"Of course not!"

"Then face facts. At one point, she will slip away from us and go confront whatever is calling to her from the ocean. Alone."

The obvious logic didn't mean Auric didn't want to punch Teivel in the face. "I don't think we should dangle her like bait."

David snorted. "You do realize this is

Muriel we're talking about, right? If she knew we were even thinking it, she'd volunteer."

The term 'fools rush in' came to mind.

"Did it ever occur to you that what's happening might not be dangerous? Remember who she is. She's tapped three parts of her magic. Who's to say her power's not craving a new type of fellow?"

Snapping on Bambi for speaking her mind would not only get him in the bad books with Chris, but it wouldn't change that she'd said aloud what Auric dreaded.

Are we about to be joined by a fourth?

CHAPTER THREE

The warm water in the deep tub didn't soothe me. Neither did the entire box of bath salts tossed into it. Nor the seashells crunching under my butt.

I craved something colder, wilder, and truly salty.

Argh. And not a pirate type 'Argh', but a frustrated one.

I submerged myself underwater, not for the first time, and blew out air bubbles of irritation. What was with this sudden obsession of mine with the ocean?

I hated the beach. Having spent most of my formative years in the pit—where heat and grit proved a constant bane—when it came to getting away, I was more into mountain retreats, winter wonderlands, places where I didn't sweat, despite the twenty-four-hour assurance on the label of my antiperspirant.

Yet, here I craved, with a need that pissed me off, the ocean. Which meant something was afoot.

Hello, chaos, my constant friend.

I rose from the layer of bubbles, a wet goddess sleek and…screaming like a little girl because Auric, hovering over the tub, stared at me and said, "And here I was hoping I'd have to do mouth to mouth."

Recovering quickly, I smiled and made sure to rise a little higher so that a certain part of my anatomy bobbed on the surface of the water. "Anytime you want to blow me, I'm more than happy to spread myself wide."

Could I add that it sounded a lot sexier and not as creepy in my head?

He laughed and flicked bubbles. "Isn't requests for blowing my line?"

"You want me to blow you? Just say when." Which might have sounded sexier if a glob of bubbles on my head hadn't suddenly slid down my forehead and hit me in the eye, whereupon I yelped. "My eye, my eye. I've got soap in my eye." Able to face down a horde of demons but blubbering like a wimp over a little sting.

As my hero, Auric dutifully wiped my face clean and, even better, didn't laugh. A good thing. He might have died. Lucky for him, I wouldn't hurt him for the smirk on his lips. Even I could admit it was kind of funny. But if he dared tell anyone about it, I'd strike in retaliation, maybe when I was blowing him.

Then I'd kiss it better.

Being a gentleman—with lusty tendencies—Auric helped me out of the tub and wrapped me in a fluffy towel. I laughed as he briskly rubbed me, his rough scrub to dry the moisture bringing my skin to life.

He wrapped the towel securely around me before sweeping me off my feet and carrying me into our bedroom. I should note it was a pretty big freaking bedroom, with a custom mattress size perfect for the occasional orgy.

What could I say? I was the type of lover who thought of their comfort so they could better please me. And please me they did, alone, together, in bed, out of it.

A sinful shudder went through me. It didn't take much to get my motor running.

I tucked my head against Auric, breathing in the scent of him. One hundred percent male. My male. Mine.

Coveting, a sin I'd learned at a young age. "I love you," I murmured.

"Love you more," he retorted.

I stiffened. "This is not a competition." A grand declaration that I followed with, "But if it were, I'd win." Because my dad taught me how to cheat.

Fair play was for those who trusted in chance. I preferred sure outcomes. In that, I was a chip off the old devil.

Auric tossed me on the bed, and oops, I lost my towel on the way. Never one to miss an opportunity, I splayed across the cover, naked, skin dewy and lips parted in invitation.

My consort's mouth tilted into a partial smile. "We really should talk."

"About what? My need to feel you inside me? My craving for your lips on my skin?"

"There's something happening, Muriel."

"You're right about that." I slid a hand down my belly and ran the tip of my finger over the damp lips of my sex.

He averted his gaze. "I'm serious,

Muriel."

"So am I." I was seriously aroused.

"Something unnatural is occurring."

"When isn't there? For once, can't I have a few months, maybe even a year, where someone isn't trying to kill me or use me?" I sighed.

"I'm not trying to kill you, but I do want to use you." How an angel could smile so naughty I'd never understand, but totally enjoyed.

My arms reached out, and I attempted my most beguiling feminine pout. "Can't we just pretend I'm normal, you're normal, and as normal people, we're going to have afternoon sex because it's fun?"

"But—"

"Please, Auric." I didn't want to discuss why I was acting so odd. I feared the answer. I wanted reassurance that some things were still the same, such as Auric's love for me.

"We really shouldn't," replied my consort, in his Mr. Respectable tone, a tone that turned teasing as he added, "but I did lock the door. Seems a shame to waste this moment of privacy."

His words were encouraging, but I enjoyed even more the fact that he yanked off his shirt before he'd finished talking.

Such a nice view. Auric might have once flown the Heavens as an angel, but he had the physique of a body-building god. Slabs of muscles, bulging biceps, that perfect vee that arrowed down below his waist into his jeans.

He put his hands on the button to his pants, and I licked my lips, anticipation making my body hum.

"So I was talking to the guys," he said as he slid the button from the loop.

"What guys?"

"David, Teivel, Chris, your sister Bambi, and your dad."

"My dad?" My eyes lost their focus, and I frowned at him. "I might have grown up in a twisted household, but even I have limits. Do you really think this is the time to be bringing up my dad?" Talk about a mood killer.

"We think there is something abnormal about your sudden urge to go on a beach vacation."

"Ya think?" I didn't hide my sarcastic lilt. My attitude was one of my best attributes, that and my long hair, of which I grabbed a strand and twirled nervously. I really did not like where this conversation appeared to be headed.

"We more than think. We know it's fucked, which is why we're going on a family vacation."

"We're what?" Forget looking sexy, I bounced to my knees.

He continued on, as if his gaze wasn't riveted by my jiggling breasts. "We leave just before dawn, as a matter of fact. Your dad has given us permission to use his villa."

"You didn't sign anything, did you?" A valid question given my demonic overlord of a father tended to put in tiny, yet critical, sub-clauses that usually gave him a person's soul.

The arched brow was the only reply I got to my question. Auric knew better than to sign anything in blood.

"Aren't you worried about taking me to the beach? If we're right, and this isn't a natural urge, then doesn't this play right into someone's plot?"

"Of course I am worried. I never like it when you're the bait."

Bait? Some women might take offense at being dangled like a tasty morsel in front of the unknown. I loved it. The fact that it had even made it into the discussion showed Auric had faith in me and my abilities.

For him, I wouldn't fail. I'd kick ass and cure this obsession with the icky ocean. But not right this minute. First, I wanted a piece of my man. A nice, long, *hard* piece.

"Strip."

"Are you giving me orders, woman?"

"Trying to." But while Teivel, the strong guy in public but submissive in private, trembled at my every command, Auric was much too alpha to allow me to control him.

But I loved to try.

"I think I'm going to keep these pants on, baby."

"That might make things a little more difficult. For you." I spread my thighs. "Since you're not dipping your wick today,

I guess I'll have to make do with your tongue." Such a shame. Not! My angel was gifted in many ways. Pleasuring me orally was just one of them.

"Then again, maybe I should take them off, so they don't get *dirty*." He purred the word as he pushed down his jeans, revealing his strong thighs, but of more interest was the cock bobbing between them.

Thick, thicker than I could wrap my hand around. How I loved his size as he stretched me and pounded me.

I crooked a finger in invitation, but he took his sweet time joining me, and when he did, his legs caged mine as he straddled me. But at least he was close enough to touch. I dragged my nails lightly down the smooth skin of his chest, starting from his pecs to the curls of his pubes. Then I grasped him.

He sucked in a breath, and his shaft pulsed in my grip. A smile curved my lips as I looked up at him. Intent green eyes met mine. He thrust his hips enough to slide his cock in my grip. He mimed fucking, all the while staring at me, arousing me. Too easily could I imagine his thick dick inside me, fucking me.

Shudder. My heated arousal and his scorching gaze caused my nipples to pucker.

"Suck them," I asked. "Please."

Such a dirty word, a word I was taught from a young age showed weakness. Yet, with Auric, I didn't feel weak. I felt desire, a burning desire for him to tease and please me.

Slowly, so slowly I could have screamed, he lowered himself until his lips brushed across my erect nubs.

"Yes." I hissed the word as I arched in invitation.

He accepted, and the hot flick of his tongue circling my erect peaks drew a moan from me. Another shiver. A cry of need as he tortured me with what he could do, but wasn't. I tried to force him to take my engorged nipple into his mouth by weaving my fingers through his hair and pulling.

As if I could budge a boulder named Auric. He took his sweet time, blowing hotly on my skin, tightening my nipples farther.

My whole body hummed with need so that, when he finally drew my nipple into his mouth, I think I came a little. I certainly felt my sex contracting, and the noises I made were completely incoherent.

The sensual assault lasted an eternity, and his lips sucked at my aureoles. His mouth pulled at my flesh. He divided his attention between both breasts until I fairly panted, mindless with enjoyment, on the brink of something even more wonderful.

And then he stopped.

"No," I mumbled, only to moan in pleasure as the tip of his shaft poked at my lips. Auric had repositioned himself. He now straddled my upper body, and his hands pushed by breasts together around his thick cock.

As he slid it back and forth in the valley, the head of his shaft in my mouth, I eagerly lapped at the head, tasting the salty flavor that pearled. He pulled back. I whimpered, eager for more. He obliged, pushing himself farther, driving his cock into my mouth so that I could eagerly suck.

Back and forth he rocked, and the

more he gasped and groaned, the more excited I became. There was something wonderful about bringing pleasure to someone, especially someone as reserved as Auric. He wasn't a guy to really let loose…except with me.

I relished these moments where he showed what he felt. Where I heard his enjoyment. So was it any wonder when he took my wondrous chew toy away I growled?

Then again, he moved away for a good reason. His hands gripped my thighs and spread them.

Despite my heavy eyelids, I opened my eyes because I loved watching him. Loved the strength of his body as he loomed over me. Loved the proud jut of his cock from his body. Desired with an insane hunger the drop that glistened on the tip.

"Gimme."

I must have said it aloud as I tried to sit up because he shook his head and said, "Don't you move, baby. I want you flat on your back."

Flat on my back with my legs in the

air and resting on his shoulders. How decadent. Almost as decadent as him smoothing that pearly drop over the head of his cock before nudging it against my moist nether lips.

He teased me with short dips into my sex. Push, stretch. Retreat. And then he did it again, just enough to drive me wild.

"Slam me," I begged.

He ignored my wishes. Heck, he moved away entirely, and I almost killed him, except he didn't go far. He just moved a little farther down the bed, enough that he could scoop my ass into his hands, lifting me and presenting me to his mouth.

"Mine," he purred against my wet flesh. So his. Forever and ever.

Then again, I would have agreed to anything the moment his mouth latched onto my sex. At the first wet stroke of his tongue, I had a mini orgasm, a shuddering, shivery delight that made me moan. But there was more to a good licking than that. Flicks of his tongue against my clit were followed by his tongue probing between my lips. He'd jab that freakishly long tongue of his inside me, wiggle it, and then go back to my clit for another flick. And just when I thought I could predict him, he'd change things up and pinch my sensitive button with his lips.

It was torture. It was awesome. It was enough to make me cry, "More!"

I got what I asked for as Auric responded, letting my ass hit the mattress, leaving his hands free to stroke my slick folds. A finger penetrated me, long and seeking. It curled at the tip, knowing how to find my G-spot. He stroked it, and my body arched in reply. Arched and prepared to come.

"Don't you dare come yet," Auric threatened.

Ever notice how being told you couldn't do something made it harder to resist? I tried. I really did, clenching my teeth, fisting my fingers in the sheets. But he set me up for failure when he inserted a second and third finger.

He could demand all he wanted, but he added in a rapidly flicking tongue to the fingers pumping me. Yeah, I couldn't hold it in. My climax hit me with the force of a train. Hard. Fast. Without any time to even cry out.

My sex contracted tightly around the fingers inside me, clenching then and wringing every possible ounce of pleasure it could. And there was a lot of pleasure. Wave after wave of it.

So intense, so wonderful, my greedy magic expanded within me, filled me to the brim, and then begged for more.

More pleasure. More!

Connected to me on such an intimate level, Auric knew what I needed, and yet, he didn't rub the swollen head of his cock to appease my magic. He rubbed me for other reasons. Lucky me, my angel had a selfish streak that also demanded satisfaction.

He fed me the thickness of his cock slowly, torturously. He stretched me and filled me and claimed me and drove me wild. But he wasn't the only one who knew how to cause insane pleasure. I clenched the walls of my sex around his inching length, fisting him tightly, tight enough that I drew a grunt from him, and even better, I felt his cock pulse.

I knew that pulse, that sign he was

very much enjoying himself. I also knew that I was tired of playing his slow, teasing game. My legs wrapped around his flanks, and my ankles locked and drew him deep. But that wasn't enough for me. I roped my arms around his neck and yanked him to me, plastering my mouth to his in a hot kiss, one that let me taste myself on him.

I didn't mind, especially since that finally stripped the last of his control.

"Muriel. My woman. My life." His growled words were swallowed by me as he began to thrust with his hips, sliding his shaft in and out, the slickness of my sex aiding his passage.

Faster. Faster. His rhythmic pace moved in time to my cries. Slamming. Pounding. Stretching.

"Harder," I panted.

He obliged, the force behind his rapid-fire strokes building my pleasure. But he didn't work alone. I met him thrust for thrust, squeezed even as he stretched.

I met his gaze, too distracted to kiss him, but loving that connection. His green eyes fairly sizzled as he pumped me.

Without any breath to say anything, I

dug my fingers into his shoulders, loving how the sweet friction of our bodies made us sweat, making everything slippery.

We both rocked and panted, on the brink. So close. Almost there. I knew the magical words to take us over. "I love you!" Did I speak them or think them? Did it matter? It was enough to push us off that edge of bliss. An intense orgasm slammed us both, reaffirming our link to one another. Filling my magical reservoir to the brim. Making my heart fairly burst with happiness and love.

Coming down from such a high was never easy or desirable. I was lucky in that Auric believed in cuddling. He held me spooned into his body, one of my favorite places to be, his face buried in my hair.

In this moment, I could relax, forget about what the world wanted from me. I pretended we were normal. A couple in love.

My happy place lasted about three minutes.

The interruption came in the form of a little voice asking, "What are you and Daddy doing?"

CHAPTER FOUR

Locked doors couldn't stand in my daughter's determined way, and since I wasn't about to explain why Auric and I were hugging naked, I yelled at her to knock before entering in the future. My admonition sent Lucinda stomping, yelling she hated me, and then I had to deal with a call from my father demanding to know why I was being a horrible mother expecting manners from his granddaughter.

I needed a vacation from life.

Go to the beach.

I kept saying no, yet it seemed dragging my feet at the butt crack of dawn the next morning wouldn't stop my determined lovers.

But I did my best. "I'm not going."

"You've nothing to worry about," David said soothingly. "We'll be around you twenty-four-seven, keeping you safe."

"I don't want to be babysat." The last thing I needed was my guys shadowing my every move, especially since I'd yet to let them see me pee. Call me old-fashioned, but I somehow worried the fact that I was a noisy splasher might affect their perception of me. As for the other type of bathroom visit, I kept a case of Poo Pourri under the sink. Every woman should have it. Now if I could only convince the guys to use it. Four bathrooms in the house and there were times none of them were safe.

And yet, despite the fact they couldn't digest food in a way that smelled like flowers, I still loved them. A miracle for sure.

"We have to go to the beach, Mommy. I wanna collect seashells," my lovely daughter announced, her smile adorably impish—and still not enough to convince me.

"Shell picking involves touching sand." Which, as everyone knew, had a devious ability to worm its way into clothes and shoes and hair. Not interested, and I told them that in no uncertain terms. "I don't want to go on a seaside vacation. You can't make me." With that final pronouncement, I flung my arms sideways and gripped the edge of the doorframe.

It always worked in cartoons, but those animated comedies never saw Auric in action. He just grabbed me around the waist and tossed me over his shoulder. Stupid, big, strong man. Super sexy, hot, big, strong man.

Once outside, standing in our roundabout driveway—which I'd insisted on because I'd bought a pair of scooters and enjoyed winging around it with Lucinda, pretending we were racecar drivers—we had to wait while Teivel sketched a portal.

The sky remained mostly dark, but hints of orange and pink touched the horizon. We had to move, and quickly, too, before my lover became a smoking-hot mess. Teivel wasted no time. The dark slit he opened, big enough for us all, provided a quick path to Hell, in this case, the ninth ring, right by the Darkling Sea.

"Let me check it out." David popped through first, the advance guard looking for danger. He popped back long enough to say, "The coast is clear." An obvious jab at word play.

"Me next!" My daughter clasped David's outstretched hand and skipped through, leaving me alone with Auric and Teivel.

"Don't make me do this." A plea that might have worked better if I'd not screamed it, along with a few physical threats to Auric's manparts.

Smack. The hard crack to my ass made me squeal, not so much in pain because I kind of enjoyed it, but I really didn't like the way he was ignoring my wishes.

"Why won't you listen to me? I don't want to go."

"Cluck." Such a sly taunt from my lover.

"Maybe we should have her Ass-Kicking Princess membership taken away for protesting so mightily," Teivel added.

"I'm not a coward. I just don't like the beach."

"You don't like the beach, but you want to know who's doing this to you. I know you, Muriel." Auric's voice lowered. "You want to get your hands on the culprit and wring his neck."

"More like chop it off," was my retort. But he was right. How well Auric knew me. No matter what I said, or my dislike of all things beachy, the truth was I kind of wanted to go through that portal so I could stand on the sandy shore and yell, "Come and get me, asshat." Curiosity and need wanted me to find out why the sea called my name. Why its cold, wet waves caressed me in my sleep.

And once I discovered the person or thing behind it, then I could bitch slap it and tell them to keep their briny overtures to themselves.

Like seriously. Leave me the fuck alone.

I didn't care if Auric and the others thought it was my magic looking to find a new guy to make a quartet. I had enough men. More than enough. Hell wasn't in danger, so screw getting another one. I didn't have enough hours in the day to handle yet another personality.

All this juggling of lovers, and a kid, was taking away from selfish me-time.

With one last smack on my ass, not because I was protesting but because Auric did so love to heat my cheeks, we went through the portal, a chilly void, bereft of life.

Except, in that split millisecond between worlds, I could have sworn I felt something. A presence. A dark and cold—

The sensation vanished as we stepped out onto the other side, the heat of Hell chasing away the shivers. Heat wasn't the only noticeable difference. My nose wrinkled as the odiferous seaside invaded it.

Earth side or Hell, the smell of the ocean was the same. The heavy-with-salt water injected the air with a moisture that left the skin salty and dried the heck out of it. Moisturizer was a must! Good thing I'd packed a few bottles.

The sand, black here along this stretch of the Darkling seashore, flowed for miles in each direction, the expanse broken only by jutting gray rocks, and a few hundred yards to our left, I grimaced at the rancid carcass of something dead—and larger than my couch back home—that washed ashore.

Decaying fish never smelled good unless you were a hellgull with charcoal feathers, bright red eyes, and a razor-sharp beak made for tearing flesh. Raucous, nasty creatures.

Auric set me on my feet on the sand, and it was almost comical the way all my men were braced and attentive to our surroundings, as if expecting something to burst from the sand and attack us. It probably didn't help that I'd thrown the movie *Tremors* on the big screen last night. I did so love me some young Bacon.

Since my tingly sense of preservation wasn't going off, I could have told my lovers they had nothing to fear. There was no danger here. Yet…

On impulse, I kicked off my thong sandals and let my toes dig into the gritty sand. It sifted warmly through my little piggies, and was it me, or did I feel an itch in my bikini bottom as a few small pieces magically wormed their way in? The invasion had already begun.

But I'd bear it because this was the place. This was where I needed to be. A sense of rightness hit me as soon as I let myself dip my feet into the water lapping the beach.

Whatever has been calling me is around here someplace.

I barely noticed when I walked farther into the rolling waves, but I did take note of the hands that kept me from wading farther.

"Let me go." I strained against those holding me back, the briny liquid lapping at my thighs, urging me to go deeper. Sink into the water. Let the waves take me…

Fuck. The insidious compulsion proved terribly strong.

"Don't let me go in there." This time I said the right words, yet my body was determined to ignore me. All of me leaned forward, craving the cold comfort of the sea.

Thankfully, I had some help fighting the crazy urge. With David on one side and Teivel on the other, I found myself lifted and marched back to the sandy shoreline.

Head canted to the side, pigtails swinging, Lucinda giggled. "Mommy looks just like the puppy when I hold him over the pool."

Indeed, much like the poor hovering hellhound that my progeny decided needed a dunking, my legs continued to churn.

"Well, at least we know we're in the right place," I announced in a voice much too cheerful. But inside, my thoughts were whirring. Why did I not feel any danger? I obviously wasn't acting of my own volition, yet no warning bells rang.

Was my body in cahoots with someone else?

Mutiny!

But how could I fight it?

Given my feet seemed determined to march to their own tune, once again, I found myself tossed over a shoulder, David's this time. An overprotective daddy called Auric held Lucinda on his hip with one arm while his other hand held his sword. As for my dark vampire knight, Teivel brought up the rear, carrying the baggage, and he didn't hide his displeasure about it.

"The shame of being reduced to a mere bellhop is almost enough to make me expire."

"Can you hold off dying until later? I've got plans."

Big plans, and no, I wasn't just

referring to the size of their equipment—which, I might add, was rather large.

The steps, chiseled into the cliff face, rose at a steep angle, their surface worn smooth by time and yet, at the same time, pitted by the elements. Gray lichen clung to some of the rock, and my guys had to tread carefully around the hellgull bombs splattered on the steps. The stuff could eat through leather and rubber so quickly that you didn't realize it until your feet started burning.

About halfway up, my feet finally started behaving, to the point that David set me down, but only for a moment to see if I'd run back to the sea. I didn't, but that didn't mean I didn't lift my arms and smile at him.

He scooped me princess-style and carried me the rest of the way. Only the truly athletic would want to torture themselves with stairs on a vacation.

And this was a vacation dammit. A much-needed one from my day-to-day life. It only occurred to me as we climbed the steps that I might not have escaped much given all the people I lived with accompanied me. We'd only changed locations.

But perhaps the change in scenery would make me a better mother and consort. If not, then at least I wouldn't have to dig a hole to bury the bodies. I'd donate them to the sea.

I had to hope, though, that this seaside break wouldn't result in murder or turn me into a veritable sea hag, although if I hit the right note when yelling, I did sound like a fishwife, according to Auric.

With comments like those, it was a wonder he lived.

When I reached the top of the bluff, a stiff breeze stroked my skin and lifted my hair. In it I could feel the sea's musical call, but I pretended to be tone deaf as I took in the surroundings.

Not much had changed since my last visit as a child. The top of the bluff was windswept rock with a few sparse attempts at sea grass growing, the yellow fronds pushing forth from between cracks in the rocks. A smoothed path led from the stairs to a weathered, wooden deck. The gray planks only creaked a little as we stepped upon them. A few lounge chairs decorated the space, not that you could really tan in Hell. The ambient light we got in daytime illuminated Hell, but didn't have the UV rays needed to change the pigment color of our skin. That simple fact was why Teivel could strut about with confidence, not fearing he'd suddenly turn into a sizzling side of beef.

Contrary to what some claimed, human flesh, even the vampire kind, did not taste like chicken.

The villa itself was constructed of shaped lava, stronger than concrete and able to withstand even the most vicious of storms that rolled in from the Darkling Sea. It rose two stories and had windows, big ones, encased within the solid black rock.

The patio doors, which ran over half the width of the house, opened at my touch, a keyless entry that recognized who I was. In Hell, mechanical devices didn't always work as they should, especially in the inner rings. Ash constantly sifted down, the fine particles jamming mechanisms. But magic, which flowed abundantly in

Hell, always worked, if you knew how to shape it and wield it.

We stepped from the deck into a wicker furniture nightmare. Whoever had originally decorated this place had a sick obsession with the stuff and then, to make matters worse, cushioned the woven shit with brightly flowered, garish cushions. It was enough to make a person's eyes bleed.

"Welcome to vacation hell," I announced as I flopped onto the settee. I should have probably warned my guys the stuff wasn't too sturdy, but they realized that quickly when David dropped onto the cushion beside me and our combined weight sent it crashing to the floor.

"Shit, sorry," my embarrassed kitty said while my sadistic daughter—who truly took after me—clapped her hands and laughed.

"Do it again!"

A good idea if it meant getting rid of the wicker, except the wicker wasn't that easily gotten rid of.

David yanked me to my feet, and I didn't have to look when he said, "What the fuck?"

I knew exactly which fuck he spoke of. Apparently, he'd just noted the indestructible nature of wicker. The couch we'd just broken sat whole once again, looking innocuous, daring us to sit on it.

Creepy stuff. My dad claimed it wasn't him who put the spell on the furniture. My personal theory was the damned furniture was cursed. Even setting it on fire couldn't destroy it.

I did have to admit, though, that my attempts to pulverize the wicker had provided hours of fun on previous visits. Don't tell my father, though. He'd be devastated if he thought I enjoyed any part of our torturous family vacations.

"So what's the plan?" I asked as I flopped again on the couch. "What kind of traps are we setting for the person pissing me off? Are we setting up mines on the beach? Conjuring a sand golem? Pulling the harpoon out of the storage shed?"

"You have a harpoon?" This from my still so delightfully innocent David.

I couldn't help a roll of my eyes. "Duh. Everyone living by the sea does on account of the monsters."

"Monsters?" Lucinda's eyes brightened. "Can I have one?"

For once I wasn't the one yelling, "no!" But I did roll my eyes when my precious darling burst into tears, forcing David and Auric to hasten to reassure her that she could get a new pet fish when we got home.

Suckers, yet I could understand their dilemma. I still remembered the tears my daughter shed when I wouldn't let her keep the cute pink dragon my daddy gave her. I did compromise, though, by allowing it to stay in my dad's stable by his palace. It was pink! Of course my baby girl had to have it. As to the fact that it was growing at a ridiculous rate and ate a few of my dad's prized hellsteeds? Maybe daddy dear would think twice next time before giving his granddaughter an enormous carnivore as a pet.

I wandered from the well-meaning daddies to the window and didn't move as Teivel brushed against my back. His chilly presence always had a soothing effect on the heat that always raged within.

"Do we have to worry about you

swan diving off the cliff into the water?" he asked.

"Should you worry that I might make you watch and not allow you to touch yourself later when we go to bed?"

The cold breath of his chuckle teased the lobe of my ear and made me shiver. "You know that's not a punishment, right?"

Indeed, I did know. My submissive vampire did so love sensual torture. "I am not planning on doing a cannonball, in reply to your question. Whatever urge possessed me below is gone."

My claim, however, didn't appease them. Apparently, they felt a need to test my earlier oddness. Armed with a few plastic buckets and shovels, along with a few towels and a lounge chair for me, we headed down to the beach. Lucinda wanted to make sandcastles, with moats and monsters.

While she happily dug around in the sand, I did my best to not touch it, lying upon the lounger and attempting to relax. Hard to relax, though, when I had three very attentive males watching my every twitch.

To their chagrin, I'm sure, I didn't attempt to drown myself in the ocean. Not a single tentacle popped from the waves. We spent the most uneventful morning and afternoon hanging on the beach, walking the shoreline. I even dipped a toe in the water.

Nothing happened. Talk about anti-climactic. Was it any wonder after we put my darling child to bed I found myself in need of some sensual excitement, the kind that came only with three lovers determined to please?

First, though, I had to convince them. Could you believe they actually wanted to hang around the kitchen table and discuss strategies?

"Strategy for what?" I interrupted finally. "We haven't seen anybody suspicious. Nothing has happened since my seawalk attempt this morning. Planning requires an enemy or target or something."

"What would you suggest we do then? Sit around and twiddle our thumbs?" Auric, ever my practical consort.

"If you need something to twiddle,

then might I suggest these?" A brazen nature meant my clothes hit the floor within a blink of an eye. I cupped my full breasts and presented them.

Auric leaned back in his chair and crossed his arms. He pretended disinterest, yet I could see the smoldering fire in his gaze. "And how does my playing with your nipples help our situation?"

I shrugged. "Never said it would help. But it sure would be fun."

David was the first to pounce from his chair. "She does have a point. This is a vacation. Fun is expected." He stood behind me and let an arm curve around my body so that he might tweak an already hard nub.

I knew I loved him for a reason. As for Teivel, he was asking for a staking when he said, "We should be staying on guard."

"Good point," Auric replied. "You can stand watch over us as we pleasure Muriel."

Before anyone got insulted on Teivel's behalf, remember this was a guy who got off on tease and denial. Watching aroused him. Knowing he watched aroused me.

The biceps on my vampire lover's arms bunched, and his eyes turned dark, blacker than a mole on a witch. "I will keep you safe while you pleasure the princess."

"If that's the case, then what is everyone waiting for? Catch me if you can." I darted from the open kitchen and living area for the bedroom I'd taken over. It wasn't as big as the master suite, but given my dad's decorative tastes, and the fact that he used that bedroom—ugh—I stuck to my room with its king-sized bed—not the custom monster-sized one I had at home, but it would have to do.

As I dove at the fuchsia quilted coverlet, I rolled so that I landed on my back instead of my stomach. A good thing, too, seeing as how a hard body landed atop mine. A naked one. David had long ago mastered the art of stripping as he sprinted.

He leaned above me, his blond hair flopping over his brow, his lips quirked in a teasing grin. "Gotcha," he announced.

"Do you?" I retorted as my hand reached between our bodies to clasp him.

The wild side of him flared, sparking his eyes. I pursed my lips in invitation, and he rewarded me with a kiss. How I loved the sensual slide of his lips on mine, the nibbles on my lower lip, the abrupt cessation as a certain consort arrived and shoved him off.

Auric might have taken his time arriving, but he, too, was now naked. Actually, the only one who wore clothing to the event was Teivel. He stood sentinel in front of the door. The whites of his eyes bled into black, a sign that the monster within him enjoyed the show, but at the same time, I knew he would guard us during our play. I licked my lips and smiled at him. My vampire lover didn't move, but through the bond that linked us, I sensed his pleasure—his hunger…

I knew all about hunger. Ever since I'd discovered sex and my magic had blossomed, it seemed I couldn't get enough. Every act fed me yet still left me wanting more.

Judging by the men flanking me, Auric on my left, hand gripped around his thick shaft, David on my right, fingers trailing up my thigh, I'd get what I needed.

Since they took too long to get going, I reached over and grabbed David's throbbing cock. Long, slender, it pulsed in my grip, yet before I could taste the moisture pearling on its tip, a rough kiss took my lips. Auric wanted some attention.

My pleasure. My mouth joined him in a nibbling battle that resulted in duelling tongues. When it came to embraces, we tended to try and dominate. Auric usually won, mostly because his forcefulness tended to ignite my passion to such an extent that I became almost mindless.

With a sharp nip to my lower lip, Auric broke the kiss and growled. "Kiss David." It never failed to excite me when Auric ordered me to touch his best friend, now also my best friend and lover. I offered my mouth to David, and he kissed me with his softer lips, his warm breath mixing with mine.

I loved the raspy feel of his tongue, not one hundred percent human and oh so delightful when used a little farther south on my body. As he embraced me, he kept sliding his hand up and down my thigh, tickling and teasing, making my sex moisten with anticipation.

And then there were two hands teasing. Auric's rougher palm dragged across my soft skin, climbing from my knee, up some more, until he dragged his fingers across my mound. A moan, a moan I couldn't help, was swallowed by David's mouth when Auric's finger found my clitoris and rubbed it.

"Yes," I hissed as he circled the swollen nub with the tip of his finger. "Touch me," I begged, yet he continued to tease me.

As if Auric tempting me weren't enough, David joined him, which meant two fingers, one from each of my lovers, enticing the flesh around my sex. It was maddening. Wonderful. It drove me utterly insane. I squirmed, knowing better than to beg, even though I needed more.

Instead of more, the hands withdrew. "No." I practically sobbed the word. How utterly evil of them to stop now. But then again, I forgave them quickly when I realized they'd stopped only so they could get more wicked.

"Grab her wrists," Auric commanded,

and David obeyed.

As my arms were pulled over my head, I caught a glimpse of poor Teivel, standing sentinel by the door, his eyes dark and glittering, the arousal so visible below his waist, and even more overpowering through our link. I knew he wanted to throw himself on me, to slide between my thighs and lap at my nectar before sinking his teeth into my tender flesh.

Some people might fear the bite of a vampire. I knew better. For someone like me, the giving of blood, especially during sex, was a heady kind of high.

But it wasn't Teivel who got to lick. While David held me prone, his grip strong and unrelenting, Auric knelt between my thighs.

"Look at me," he ordered.

I couldn't disobey. I gazed at him through eyes heavy with passion. Watched as he spread my legs wide, exposing me. Some women might feel vulnerable to have not one but two men staring at their pinkness, seeing the quiver in the moist flesh. I reveled in it. Craved it.

Look upon me. Desire me. Touch me. Even

better, taste me.

My unspoken words seemed to act as a trigger as Auric fell upon me, his tongue finding my silken slit and stroking. The exquisite feel of him lapping saw me arching, but not far. David pushed me down, pinned me with his body, and held me prisoner for their desire.

I gasped as I gazed upon the dark hair of my lover between my thighs. His face buried, Auric didn't just lick me with finesse. He enjoyed it, too. He hummed against my flesh and rumbled pleased moans, the rhythmic vibration raising my excitement.

I moaned aloud a few times, too, until David took my lips, swallowing my sounds of pleasure. But my lips were no match for my aching nipples. They pointed straight into the air and begged for some attention. David latched onto a tight nipple, sucking the peak into his mouth, drawing a scream from me with it.

The dual sensations proved too much. My body bucked from the bed as my arousal peaked and crested. I screamed as I exploded, the waves of my climax rolling through me, again and again. Yet they still weren't done.

Lucky me.

A naughty kitty, David bit down on my nipple. I let out a mewl of enjoyment, and a quiver rocked me as the little jolt of pleasure-pain zinged to my pussy. Auric sucked on my quivering nether lips, drawing another moan and a gasped, "More."

It was painful ecstasy, yet I didn't want them to stop.

"I'll give you more," Auric growled against my sex, the hot words making my sensitized flesh clench.

It took some manhandling, but in a moment, I found myself straddling Auric, the tip of his cock brushing against my swollen sex. How delightfully decadent.

Placing my hands on his chest, I leaned slightly forward, the soft brush of my hair sliding over my bare shoulders teasing my sensitized breasts. David placed his hands on my waist and pushed me downward. Slowly, he controlled my descent, each inch drawing Auric's cock deeper into me. The width of him, as usual, never failed to stretch me. Please me. How tight it felt. So good.

I loved how Auric never closed his eyes when we made love. His intense green gaze always watched me. Seeing the heated intensity never failed to excite. But it was his murmured, "Fuck me but I love you," that saw my pussy clenching tightly.

It never failed to awe me that these men loved me. They saw past my flaws, and they embraced my uniqueness. With them, I was someone special. And they showed me in so many ways.

Their love for me, and mine for them, was a power all its own, one that enhanced our sexual play, which, in turn, heightened not only my arousal but also the flavor of my magic.

All of me hummed. And hungered. This slow, sensual easing of myself onto Auric's shaft was taking too long. I wanted all of him, now. My nails dug into his chest, bracing me, and despite David's attempt to control me, I pushed, pushed down with all my strength, slamming the rest of Auric's cock into me.

I gasped, Auric grunted, and I wasn't

alone in reacting. My pussy quivered, and in turn, Auric's cock spasmed. Yum.

With a wiggle of my hips, I rocked against him, the sharp jolt of pleasure making my nails dig deeper. Again, I gyrated, feeling my pleasure mount, getting to that peak that never failed to please me.

"Not yet," Auric growled. "Teivel, toss over the lube."

Lube? It was going to be that kind of night?

My vampire watcher did more than toss over the oily gel. He dribbled it down the crack of my ass with an approving David saying, "Slick her up. I like it greasy."

Indeed he did, and I loved it, too. The swollen head of David's cock poked at my rosette. I didn't flinch or tighten. I knew what to expect.

I leaned forward farther, driving Auric deep while spreading my ass cheeks wide, giving David even better access. The cap of his shaft popped into me with ease, yet my sex still contracted, something Auric reacted to with a hiss.

And then the real fun started.

Anyone who's been sandwiched

between two men knows the taboo pleasure of having two bodies rubbing, skin to skin. Of having two dicks buried deep. It was distracting. Amazing. Mind blowing. I didn't know who was doing what. Who was coming or going. All I truly knew in that moment was it felt so fucking good.

There was a special kind of rhythm to this type of lovemaking, one that they controlled. While Auric thrust in, David pulled out. When Auric withdrew, David thrust in. I just gasped and moaned as they took me for a ride.

I'd closed my eyes when they started, but Auric didn't approve. "Open your eyes."

I did and trembled at Auric's green gaze. But it wasn't him I was supposed to watch. "Look sideways."

Turning my head, I noted Teivel, standing alongside the bed, lube in one hand, fully dressed and watching. Suffering. Needing…

"Unbutton your pants," I ordered.

How fast a vampire could move when motivated. His long and thick cock, color of the whitest marble, sprang forth, the tip of it swollen yet not blushed with color, not like my other lovers.

As a pair of cocks drove into me, matching their cadence so I was filled at the same time, I panted but managed to say, "Oil it. Then stroke it. Stroke it for me."

No other urging was required for him to dribble the liquid onto his shaft, the oily fluid making his cock glisten. Then his hand gripped it, stroking it back and forth, gliding with ease, the strokes slow. But I knew he enjoyed it. I could see it by the tightness of his sac, the rigidity of his pose.

"Come closer," I beckoned. "Closer."

He brought it close enough that I could blow warm air on it. And I did, loving how it made him shudder. I could do nothing else, though, nothing but cry out as Auric and David pumped me harder. Faster. They pistoned me, one sinking deep while the other withdrew. Back in, balls-deep, out. Freaking awesome.

My body tensed and then exploded, drawing a long scream from me, one that was cut short as Teivel thrust himself into my mouth. I suckled him greedily, eating his yummy cock while Auric and David fed my ass and sex their own throbbing dicks. As Teivel spurted into my mouth, so did they spurt, too, the hotness of their cream triggering a second orgasm on top of the first.

My magic swelled. My heart did, too. And happier than the damned cat who'd eaten the canary, I collapsed in a happy heap of naked limbs and sweaty skin.

CHAPTER FIVE

The tickle of moonlight on bare skin woke me, but it was only as I stretched to fully enjoy its cold, silvery embrace that I realized a few crucial things.

One, there was no moonlight in Hell. Ever. The pit resided in some strange pocket universe without the constellations of the mortal world.

Crucial point number two. My body didn't lounge on a bed with soft-as-sin sheets and a memory foam mattress. Fuck, I wasn't even in the villa anymore.

And the third important point, which truly made me simmer, there was bloody sand in my unmentionables, probably because I was lying on the beach at the bottom of the bluffs wearing just a T-shirt that I'd flung on before wandering to the bathroom for some middle of the night business. No panties, though. I'd had too many of them torn off for urgent morning sex—by me—to waste a pair.

Last, but not least, not only did I find myself not in bed, on a beach with no idea how I'd gotten there, there were also no consorts watching over me. That never happened. And I certainly never expected it on this trip, not given their plan to dangle me as bait.

Given all these items, was it any wonder I felt a touch perturbed? My hand also itched for a certain Hell blade, left lying in the bedroom, leaning against the nightstand. Auric had brought my blade along for me. Apparently he didn't trust me with it when they dragged me here. As if I would maim them. I liked their body parts too much to lop any off.

From now on, I'm sleeping with a dagger strapped to my thigh.

Despite my weaponless state, I remained far from helpless. I still could rely on my impressive fighting skills as well as my magic, both of which I would wield better if I wasn't taken unaware. That meant no more using the beach as a bed. I scrambled to my feet, my toes squishing in the damp sand. The tide had washed out, and before anyone asked, no one knew how the tides worked on this plane without a moon. It was one of those things we just took for granted, like the creamy filling in those yummy eggs at Easter. I didn't understand how that worked either, but that didn't prevent me from eating one. Okay, I ate two. Argh. Fine. I admit it. I liked to buy a box and devour them while watching corny chick flicks.

Don't judge. My dad knows about all your naughty habits. Your file is pretty thick, which is probably why we'll get along when you come join us in the pit.

But we could worry about your eventual relocation later. Right now, we needed to worry about me. Given my previous problem when we arrived, I did have some concern that I might start marching off to sea again. I glanced about for something to grab hold of before my feet mutinied. Alas, nothing appeared for me to anchor myself, and I might have worried except, for the moment, my body seemed to be listening to me and not dancing to its own tune. Awesome.

Less awesome was the fact that I'd found myself on the beach in the first place. How had that happened? Had I walked? Been carried? Did I dream?

Last I recalled, my boys and I had made it to a bed, a bed that could have used a few more feet of mattress. But we'd made do. Things got pretty hot and steamy. The aftereffects still filled my magical reservoir. I fairly burst with power, which made me cocky and, in turn, totally erased any fear a normal person might have felt.

If any nasty sea monsters try and take me, I'll pulverize them into chunks of sushi.

Confidence was my best friend and fear not an emotion I liked to entertain. The situation might appear creepy, but I found myself intrigued. The shaft of light, a brilliance not projected by any moon but shining directly from the umber-hued night sky, didn't worry me. I saw it for what it was. A cheap parlor trick meant to enhance the shape emerging from the waters.

A curious cat, like David, might have succumbed to staring. Auric would have indulged in direct confrontation. Teivel enjoyed hanging back and then swooping for maximum effect. Show off. Could you tell I envied his style?

Paying it attention would have given it too much credit. I opted for feigned disinterest. My gaze went to my skin, my poor abused skin covered in a patina of sand. Gross. I proceeded to slap myself—while mentally humming a certain Britney Spears song—free of the icky, clinging sand. Such nasty, gritty stuff. I took my sweet time about it.

Nonchalance at its finest. Given I wasn't going to give the approaching intruder the attention he craved, I guess I could spend a moment explaining parts of my method. Because while half of me thought it was a great idea, the other half of me, the part in touch with my humanity and sense of self-preservation, screamed I was an idiot.

Maybe I was. A more concerned person, at the imminent approach of an unknown in an extreme situation, might have run and called for help.

I think we'd all seen how that movie ended. The girl died, usually in some horrible, slimy way. Like fuck. And no thank you. A coward ran, and there was nothing yellow about my belly. But I really needed to work on my tan.

Another reason to not scream for help was that it might bring my boys. They were adorably protective of me, but that also worked in reverse. What if the approaching enemy—enemy, yes, because in my world that was how it worked—hurt my dear lovers? *Hurt them and I will kill you.*

Harm my child? *And I will rip your guts from your body and feed them to you before staking you to feed the carrion birds.*

What if it was after me?

I should be so lucky. A girl did so enjoy a chance to practice her skills. I'd perfected the bitch slap and had started a video collection of the expressions on assassins' faces when I delivered it. It had been days since I'd added a new image.

So many reasons to stay and fight instead of seeking out allies. Until I better understood what we faced, I would investigate it alone—and reap the benefits of punishment later.

Bad girls did sometimes win.

Even with my partial attention, I noted a few key points about the approaching sea invader. One, he definitely was coming for me. Two, he was human-appearing so far, with two legs and arms, a head, a torso, and because he was also naked, I couldn't help but note he was hung like a seahorse. Or was that a whale? I never could get my aquatic creatures straight, even though I'd hung out with a kid who knew everything.

When young, my playmate Adexios, Charon's son, used to mock my lack of knowledge. So I knocked out his front teeth then hid because I was terrified his mom would kill me. Can you say mama's boy? But his mom didn't kill me and dismember my body. Apparently, I saved them a bundle in dental fees, and Adexios, that jerk, got a tidy bundle from the tooth fairy. So unfair.

When I lost baby teeth, my father had them ground, put in some kind of magical milkshake, and I had to chug it while hopping on one foot counterclockwise. Something about making sure I didn't leave anything behind for my enemies to use against me. Although the videos Daddy took as I wobbled, feeling like a moron, made me wonder if he wasn't pulling one of his practical jokes. One never knew with the devil.

It seemed a little too stubborn, even for me, to pretend I didn't watch the water dude's approach, given he was close enough that the very air around me vibrated.

Power. Coming from him. My insidious inner self, linked tightly with my magic, purred the thought. Urged me to move closer and touch. Take.

Yummy. We should make him ours.

Bad thought. Where did it come from? Why was it proving so insistent? Just what was so freaking great about this guy? I had to see. Therefore, I pivoted and faced him full-on, hands on my hips, head angled at its most disdainful princess angle. It was a great look, practiced many hours in front of a mirror. It should have evoked some kind of response. My favorite was the trembling, sometimes accompanied by puddles at their feet. The knee drop where they blubbered for my forgiveness. Yet this guy didn't act as expected. Instead, he retaliated in the worst way possible at my most evil stare.

He dared to grin back and look drop-dead sexy doing it. The world under my feet tilted. I would swear something shifted. And this man, creature, hunk of sex on two legs, was the cause.

Uh-oh.

A red glow entered my eyes as I ensured my irritation—and, yes, a little bit of panic—lit them with the flames I'd inherited from my father.

The sea dude didn't slow his step—his long-legged, fluidly graceful step.

Gulp.

Look away. Look away. I needed to resist.

What a joke. I was a bad girl for a reason. I wanted to look and ogle and admire. Once I'd made that decision, I subjected him to the once-over. My gaze started at his feet—*my what big feet you have*—rose to check out corded calves—the better to brace yourself—thick, muscled thighs—that could probably piston for hours—skipped past a certain proud mast—*so in the mood for a Popsicle right now*—to a flat belly with—

"You have no belly button?" For

some reason that struck me as oddly freakish, and I giggled.

That got a reaction. My deadliest glare had done nothing, but my mirth at his condition did cause the water dude to slow his step, and as I chuckled louder, he stopped.

"Are you laughing at me?" His voice proved as sexy as the rest of him. The hole being dug beneath my feet got deeper.

I needed to not topple in. Disengage and move away. That didn't happen. Now, when I needed my feet to move me away from this strangely alluring fellow, they remained stuck to the ground as if weighted by cement blocks. I well remembered the feeling, the time my dad got me back for shoving rocks in his favorite loafers—trimmed in rhinestones— and turning them into a coral reef for his tropical, rainbow-colored piranhas. Only tanks of the purest diamond glass could hold those vicious critters. My dad's shoes were gone in seconds. As punishment, Dad sank me in the hot springs in the lava rock garden, but on the upside, I found my missing earring.

The blast from my past was nice, but I recognized it as an attempt to avoid my attraction to the hot guy with no belly button. "Yes, I was laughing at you. Still am," I added with a smirk. "But isn't that better than pitying you? I mean, look at you, you're missing a hole. It's so weird."

A good thing, too, that he possessed some kind of flaw because the rest of him was pure-platinum perfection. Once I got past his bodily sexiness—with difficulty—I noted his square, clean-shaven jaw, his aquiline nose, sharp cheekbones, full sensual lips, and long, really fucking long, platinum hair.

His chin angled at an imperial tilt I knew well as he replied, "I am not missing anything. Only mammals have umbilical cords."

"So what are you, a fish?" He didn't look like one. No tail, fins, gills, or scales.

"I am Poseidon's son."

Poseidon, also known as Neptune or the god of the sea. I knew him well since he was my daddy's drinking and wenching buddy. But I'd never met his son. "Neptune's boy, eh? With who? Doesn't matter, I guess, you're still a fish."

He frowned, but still managed to look utterly delicious. I almost made the sign of an inverted cross.

"I am not a fish but a merman."

A snicker that was part snort left me. "A merman? Do I look that fucking stupid? You can't be a merman because they don't exist."

"I beg to differ since we do. I take it you've heard of mermaids."

Did the roll of my eyes properly convey my 'Duh'? I restrained an urge to slap him—then kiss him better. "I know all about mermaids, enough to know there are no male ones." No one quite understood the whole biology thing with them, but I did know that they came in the feminine version only. The few male progeny they birthed were vicious sea monsters without any kind of human characteristics.

"Mostly true except for the fact that I exist, but I will admit I'm rare."

"Understatement by the guy with no belly button." But really nice abs. The unblemished skin truly wanted stroking. I held my hands clasped, lest they wander off to play. "I'm surprised you don't get that fixed."

His brows drew into a sharp V. "Would you stop it already with the belly button thing. You do not see me mocking you."

"What's there to mock?" I swept my hands in a show of my body that I knew he liked because a certain part of him bobbed for attention. I ignored it in punishment—to myself. "I am flawless, as you can see. Awesome. Brave. Cunning. And I could go on. There's a whole alphabet created to describe me."

"Is L longwinded because this conversation seems to have no end. I have better things to do than wait for you to get to the point."

Something better than verbally sparring with me? Talk about insulting. "I'm not sure what point you want me to make other than keep your weird sea shit to yourself. No more of those dreams you've been sending. Or the marching feet. Or the sex stuff."

"Sex stuff? Feet? Dreams?" His brows arched. "What insanity are you spouting? Have you smoked some kelp?"

"Don't play innocent." I wagged my finger at him. "I know all about the stuff you've been doing to get me here on this beach. And I am telling you to stop."

"I did nothing to get you here. You were the one who called me. I heard your message in the waves and curiosity made me come to see what it was about."

"I called you?" I shook my head. "No. You started this, and I want to know why you've been invading my dreams and making me crave the ocean. It's really not nice, especially considering I can't stand seafood." Although, given he did appear quite appetizing, I might make an exception in his case.

I didn't need my father cringing in disgust to know the guy spoke the truth when he said, "I assure you, it was not I invading your dreams, but you were commandeering mine. And I demand that you stop."

"No, you stop."

"No, you."

"You."

"You."

It might have gone on for a while if, with every yell, we hadn't taken a step closer and closer and closer until the last word was swallowed in a kiss.

Oh dear.

Oh yes.

His soft lips slanted over mine, and my awareness blossomed, a new part of me awakening and unfolding much like the petals on a flower kissed by morning sun. My senses opened and drew in a wondrous new essence, one with the crisp, cool of water, the salty tang of the sea, and a wildness of crashing waves.

I wanted more. More. More—

He broke the kiss and stepped away, his breathing harsh, his eyes glittering. "What are you? Who are you?"

How could he not know? Was my marketing team truly not tapping all the markets, including the aquatic ones? I drew myself up, every inch of me regal, even in my T-shirt that said, Delicate Freakn' Flower. "I am Satana Muriel Baphomet."

While he might not have recognized the face, he knew the name. "The devil's daughter. Fuck."

And with those words, water dude spun on a heel and ran back to the waves. I might have protested his hasty departure except the view of his flexing buttocks proved quite hypnotizing. I stared at the rolling waves long after he disappeared from sight, and I might have stared longer had I not heard a bellow.

"MURIEL!"

It seemed Auric found out I was gone, and the tinkle of glass let me know someone wasn't happy about it.

CHAPTER SIX

"Muriel!" Again I heard the sweet, bellowed sound of my name. No matter how many times my angelic consort might yell, it never failed to tickle me. I trained my gaze to the sky, once again dark, as the mysterious light vanished with my sea visitor.

Still, being half demonic gave me some ability, and with a flick of my hand, a faint luminance lit the sky overhead. A sea breeze lifted a tendril and teased it past my cheek, yet I didn't allow it to distract me from the aerial predator gliding on a current, arrowing rapidly toward me. My fallen angel approached upon shadowy wings, sporting a fearsome scowl.

I waved. "Hi, honey." It seemed stupid to pretend I wasn't there. He'd obviously noticed my absence in bed. The least I could do was reassure him. "I'm okay." Then drive him crazy. "The guy you're looking for went that way." I pointed toward the mockingly calm ocean.

A roar of rage was the reply as my angry angel banked on his gossamer wings of gray, crisscrossing the still sea, looking for a merman long gone.

And what would you have done if your sea visitor had stayed? Auric would have gone after him for sure. He'd gotten so protective since the debacle with Lilith. He might have ripped into the merman without asking questions. The thing I had to wonder was, what would I have done? A part of me seemed to think I would have intervened. For a stranger?

Not a stranger if he's mine.

With thoughts like that lurking about, it was best the stranger had left. Better for us both, seeing as how calming Auric down took some doing. I caught some of his cursing. The words carried to me on the light sea breeze.

"I can't believe we were taken unawares. Fuck! Fuck!" He whistled through the air, seeking something to vent on. But there was just little ol' me, and even the thrust of my bare butt in the air didn't tempt him for a spanking.

Sighing, I straightened and let the hem of my shirt cover me. If I wasn't going to get some angry sex, or any sex, then enough already. I had sand that needed rinsing from unmentionable parts. "Are you done having a tantrum?"

"No." A sulky fallen angel was sexier than it sounded. My rebuke, though, did have an effect, as he finally decided to land. With a flutter of his wings, Auric hit the beach with two bare feet, wearing only a pair of men's boxers. Yummy. I didn't bother to hide my interested stare.

The muscles across his chest and shoulders flexed as his shadow wings retracted, pulling into his back. I didn't understand how the magic for them worked. When they appeared, they were solid to the touch, and yet, for all their massive size, once Auric put them away, so to speak, you couldn't tell he had wings at all.

"Oh, baby, I'm over here," I sang with a wave.

Only a dozen feet away from me, yet Auric didn't take a step in my direction. If I were any other kind of girl, I might have taken offense at the fact that he didn't envelop me in his arms and exclaim his happiness over finding me safe. But I was a princess of Hell. I understood danger just like Auric did.

Auric was a warrior, which meant his first priority was to assess the situation. He'd scouted from above, and now he scouted on the ground, all his senses still on high alert.

Getting bored of the posturing, I buffed my nails on my shirt and blew on them. It didn't help my chipped nail polish—the beach was harsh on manicures—but it did show my state of mind.

"Don't you play blasé with me," he growled. "This is serious, Muriel. How do you think I felt when I woke up to find you gone?"

"Not my fault you're a heavy sleeper."

"I'm not!" If he could have, he would have blown smoke his anger simmered so hot. "Something kept me, all of us, asleep."

"Weird." It also explained why it had taken him that long to come find me.

"That's all you've got to say? Weird? How about irresponsible? What were you thinking? How many times do I have to warn you against acting rashly?"

He thought I'd done this? "Don't blame me for this one. I'm innocent." I swear I felt a drop of snow as Hell suffered a sudden temperature drop at my stretching of the truth. Innocent wasn't a word I could use often, unless unjustly accused. Again, a rare occurrence. Most of the time, I was guilty. Except in this case. "I woke up on the beach with no idea how I got there."

"You sleep-walked?"

"Maybe. I don't know. All I know was I awoke lying in the sand, all alone." I batted my lashes for sympathy, only to find myself ignored.

Auric spun around and peeked at the beach, still illuminated by the light I'd called. He knelt at the spot in the sand where I'd left a Muriel-sized indentation. "I see only your steps leaving this spot. But none arriving." His brow furrowed. "Did you portal in?"

I planted my hands on my hips. "I

told you it wasn't me. It must have been *him*."

That caught his attention, and his head whipped up as he narrowed his gaze on me. "Who is this guy you've referred to twice? Where is he? Who is he?"

I shrugged. It seemed more expedient.

"Did you talk to him?" Auric asked.

"A little." And I'd kissed him, but I wasn't sure confessing right now was a good idea. Then again…the road to adventure was paved with good intentions gone bad. "We mostly argued about who was haunting who, and then we made out."

Honesty, such a powerful weapon in the wrong hands. In this case, my telling him the truth acted like an emotional nuke. Auric reeled as if injured.

It wasn't anything he would ever admit to. My fallen angel was old school when it came to expressing any emotions he considered emasculating. Yet, the tenseness in his posture, and the deeply connected bond between us, meant I felt his agitation. His jealousy. His fear. A fear he'd lose another part of me.

Never.

Forget waiting for him to approach me. I ran to him. My arms wrapped around his upper body, and for a moment, he held himself rigid before hugging me back, his arms tight bands around me.

"You will never lose me," I whispered against his bare chest. "You own my heart. You gave me a soul." Because I was pretty sure before I'd met Auric I hadn't had a proper one.

"You are my world."

The declaration was mushy sweet, and I loved it. Loved him.

I lifted my face, my lips seeking his. We clung together for a moment, two bodies and minds meshed as one, so of course, reality intruded with a shouted, "Did you find her?"

My dark vampire's query broke the kiss as Auric replied, "I've got her. Be up in a minute."

I stroked Auric's bristled cheek as his gaze returned to mine. "I'm surprised they didn't come down with you," I noted.

"They wanted to, but we didn't want to leave Lucinda unguarded. And we couldn't be sure we'd find you on the beach. So David was left to guard our little girl while Teivel searched the grounds."

How my life had changed in the past months. I no longer had just myself to worry about. I had a family, a whole bunch of them who worried and depended on me. "I wasn't in any danger." Even now, I still believed that.

"Then how did you get here?"

Good question, one that I didn't have an answer for. I clung to Auric as he swept me into his arms, his gray wings exploding from his back in a shower of gossamer feathers. With a mighty leap, he sprang into the air, flapping his wings hard, lifting us aloft.

How I loved these rare moments when we got to fly, racing on the air currents, swooping in the sky, getting dropped.

"Eek!" I squealed as I tumbled down into a waiting set of arms.

Teivel cast a sardonic gaze on me. "That was a pretty girly reaction."

I tossed my disheveled hair. "In case you haven't noticed, I am a girl."

His cool lips found the lobe of my ear, and I shivered as he whispered, "But I much prefer it when you're an evil vixen."

Shudder. If I had more time, I would have totally shown him how evil, yet Auric landed, David appeared in the door, and dawn lightened the sky.

When Auric started making breakfast—which started with a strong pot of coffee—I didn't argue. Then again, I didn't have time since I was interrogated by my other two men, with Auric piping in for good measure.

Since I couldn't avoid it, I told my boys what happened. It really wasn't much, and by the end of my tale, they were just as baffled as me.

"So he says he wasn't the one sending you the subliminal messages?" David asked.

"Lying obviously," Auric retorted.

I shook my head. "I don't think so. I've got a pretty good radar when it comes to fibs, and as far as I can tell, he was getting the same kind of weird shit happening to him as I was."

"But if he's not to blame, who is?"

Teivel interjected as he stole the last piece of bacon from David's reaching fingers and handed it to me.

My smile and wink let him know his gift wouldn't go unrewarded.

"Did someone call him in the hopes he'd kill you?" Auric mused.

Bacon gone, I debated licking the grease from the empty plate. Deciding the mockery wasn't worth it, I replied instead. "Like I told you already, I didn't get any bad vibes from the merdude. Despite the circumstances, I don't think he meant me any harm."

"I don't understand why you feel a need to defend him. He was obviously up to no good," Auric snapped.

"Perhaps he planned to kidnap you?" Teivel cracked his knuckles.

"Then why didn't he? He could have." Yet he'd chosen rather to abandon me and return to the ocean, the jerk.

"What of the kiss?" my vampire tossed out.

Teivel's query hung in the air. I'd kind of told Auric about it, but avoided telling the others. Living with a bunch of supernatural guys, though, meant not much got past them. I squirmed in my seat as their gazes zeroed in on me.

"What of the kiss? It was two lips touching. No big deal. He never even copped a feel." The rejection still galled. I could now see why the Red Queen was known for chopping off heads.

"Don't tell me Poseidon's son follows a righteous path?" Auric's incredulity colored his words.

A snicker left me. "A pious son? That would mean the apple fell really far from the tree, given Neptune's reputation for being a bit of a manwhore."

Leaning against the counter, Teivel remarked, "Are we even sure the fellow you met on the beach is Neptune's son? My lord Lucifer never mentioned the sea god as having any progeny."

"What's progeny mean?" The query came from a blonde cherub who'd wandered into the kitchen wearing a pink nightgown and rubbing sleep from her eyes with a chubby fist.

I tugged her onto my lap for a snuggle and answered. "Progeny are people's kids."

"Oh. Cool." Then because Lucinda was a child, her mind veered off in a strange direction. "Did Tristan show you his palace, Mommy?"

In the midst of cutting up some leftover pancakes for her, I paused and blinked at my daughter. I think we all did.

I asked, "Who is Tristan?"

"The man in the sea. The one you met last night."

So far, nothing too freaky. Lucinda could have eavesdropped and found that out easily. "What does Tristan look like?" Because that was one thing I'd not really gotten into.

"He's got really long, blond hair, longer than yours, Mommy. He's Neptoon's son." She beamed. "He swims with hellphins." The pit's version of a dolphin except redder, sporting a jagged razor-sharp fin and even deadlier teeth.

I couldn't be sure about the swimming with the fishies thing. The guy seemed pretty alive to me, but other than that, she'd described my nighttime visitor. "How do you know about this Tristan?

Has he been here? Did he talk to you?" Perhaps she was mixing a character from a fantasy story or movie with real life.

"No, silly." My little imp grinned, popping that dimple, but I didn't let it sway me from my line of questioning.

"Has he threatened you?" This from Auric, who'd left his spot at the stove flipping pancakes to kneel by Lucinda's chair. "If he's scared or done anything to you, Daddy will kill him."

Auric would also get his rocks polished if he kept being so darned overprotectively cute.

"Tristan is nice. Mommy is going to like him, too."

"No, Mommy's not," I muttered, slipping into the third person.

"Silly Mommy. Great-auntie Fate says you're meant to be. But it was taking too long, and the big bad thing is coming, so I made it go faster."

Wow, so many things in one sentence. Where to start?

Auric focused on one. "What do you mean, you made it go faster?"

"I sent Mommy dreams so she'd go

to the beach."

My eyes widened. "You did that? Not him?"

"Me. Me. Me," she sang. "And I sent a message, in a bottle." Lucinda clapped her hands. "A magic bottle. It told Tristan to come to the beach."

Pieces began to click into place. "But how did I get there?"

"I opened a door for you, Mommy. But it wasn't easy." My daughter scowled at her daddies and Teivel. "They were snuggling you. With no clothes." Her nose wrinkled. "I think I am going to buy you pajamas for Christmas."

Giving my lovers clothing to hide their perfection? What an evil idea. I could have wiped a tear in pride. She was so definitely my daughter.

"So let me get this straight," Auric said, his voice calm, deceptively so. I could feel the tension thrumming within him. "You were the one who gave your mom an urge to come to the beach. And then you called this sea creature."

"He's a merman, Daddy," Lucinda corrected.

"And you made sure your mom was there to meet him."

She nodded.

"Why?"

"Because he's going to be daddy number four."

CHAPTER SEVEN

Kids say the damnedest things, Auric knew that, but to hear his own daughter—*my flesh and blood*—claim she was getting a fourth daddy wrenched something in him. He left during the turmoil of Muriel shrieking, "No way," and David rushing in to calm Lucinda, who cried big tears because she'd upset Mommy.

She'd also upset Daddy, but he didn't let her see, choosing to flee rather than face his greatest fear. Another man.

How many more would come? Auric loved Muriel with all his being. He understood her magic needed more than just him, but how much more could he take?

Outside, the reddish haze of Hell painted the world in oranges and reds, except for the dark rocks and the roiling sea. He leaned against the weathered railing, staring at the frothing whitecaps, wondering if this new mer-fellow lurked.

Didn't Muriel say something about a harpoon? Perhaps he could take care of this interloper before things went too far. Before he had to share yet another piece of her.

"Jealousy? What a wasted emotion." Teivel's observation earned him a raised middle finger over his shoulder. The vampire laughed instead of taking offense. "Touchy, touchy. Did I strike a nerve?"

In times past, Auric wouldn't have spoken. He would have borne his emotions stoically, but that had been when he was alone. Now, Auric shared his life with others. Keeping things bottled or secret only made them worse.

Tension marking all of his muscles, Auric clenched the rail. "I know I shouldn't be jealous. Muriel loves me, and at this stage, what's one more guy? I mean, David came along, and we survived. You butted in, and things worked out." Better than expected actually. "Why does the thought of this new dude freak me out?"

"Perhaps because we are one step closer to seeing her ascend into her power. The knowledge that, after Tristan, there will be others. Multitudes I would wager for someone like Muriel, who is destined for great things."

Not exactly the answer he wanted. He muttered a bleak, "Where does it end?"

"It doesn't." Teivel came to stand beside him, staring out at the same featureless sea. "More will come."

"Easy for you to say. You've not lived through this twice already. Aren't you worried that something might change?"

"For an angel, you worry an awful lot. And for nothing. While Muriel might have found herself drawn to me and David and this Tristan, her love for us does not even come close to the love she has for you. We are her lovers. You are her life. She needs you."

"And I need her," Auric repeated quietly. "So what are you advocating?"

"Obviously there are forces at work determined that Muriel join with this mer-creature."

"That force is called Lucinda," Muriel said with a snort as she slid in between them. Her arm slid around Auric's waist, her other arm around Teivel's. "I don't care what she or my Aunt Fate think. I have enough men in my life, and I won't be taking another."

Was it only Auric, or did he hear the ominous cackle of a certain nosy aunt as she said, *"We'll see about that."*

"Don't you dare meddle with me or my family, old woman." Muriel shook her fist at the sky. "I'm not afraid to go to that mountain and beat your scrawny ass."

"I'd like to see you try."

Lightning quick, Auric wrapped an arm around her waist before Muriel acted, but he wasn't quick enough that afternoon to save her from the jaws of fate.

CHAPTER EIGHT

In retrospect, I should have probably listened to Auric when he said he wanted to pack our things up and head back home. Apparently, his idea to dangle me as bait didn't appeal now that he knew it was a man and not a monster we had to face, yet it wasn't Lucinda's noisy tears that convinced me to stay.

Blame my adorably stubborn nature. "I'm not leaving." I stomped my foot, which might have proven more impressive if I hadn't been lounging on a deck chair at the time pretending to tan.

"Why not?" Auric glared at me. "You hate the beach."

"I do hate it. However, Lucinda loves it, and I won't cut short our vacation because of some dude."

"That *dude* wants something from you."

I peeked at him over the rim of my sunglasses. "Well, duh. I mean, who wouldn't want a piece of this?" My hands fluttered over my scantily clad body. Modesty was for those who didn't love their curves.

My words only deepened his scowl. "I thought you didn't want that merman."

"I don't, and he's not the reason I want to stay."

"Then let's go."

"No. And nothing you say will make me change my mind. I won't have people making decisions for me. Not you, not my aunt, and certainly not my magic. We came here for a relaxing bloody vacation, and by all that is unholy, we will have one!" By the time I'd finished yelling, a little steam wisped from my nose.

Oh dear, more of Daddy's bad habits seemed to be surfacing. Luckily for Auric, he didn't remark upon it. Teivel did, and his Puff the Magic Dragon comment saw me sucker-punching him in the nut sac. His fault for standing nearby and not properly gauging my reach.

As Teivel sucked in a wheezing breath he didn't need, I stared daggers at Auric.

He didn't drop to the ground sporting bloody wounds, but he did look as if he'd swallowed a lemon. "I forbid you from staying."

Forbid me? He did not just say that. Someone pick up my jaw from the ground. "I'm not leaving, and you can't make me." I stuck my fingers in my ears and hummed. That always drove him bonkers.

What it didn't usually do was get him to draw a sword. Had I finally crossed a line with him? Was he about to go all angel seeking redemption and chop off the head of the devil's daughter?

Swish. Swing. Ew. The green ichor from the severed tentacle sprayed me and my white bikini. I needed club soda, stat, but all I had in my glass was rum and cola. No time to switch drinks, though. We had a situation at hand.

I took stock of the situation—about to get messy—and barked orders—because I loved to take command. "David, take Lucinda inside and put on your kitty. Auric, distract that monster for a second, would you? Dazzle it with your righteous angel routine. You"—I stabbed my finger at my brooding vampire—"get me some spot remover before this stain sets." I still had hope I could save my precious outfit.

As for me, I rose from my seat, in my slimy spotted bathing suit, cracked a few knuckles, and snarled, "Bring it, creature from the deep."

Yeah, mental note to self. Don't say bring it to a sea monster with dozens of tentacles. Nothing worse than having them whip out of the ocean, waggle over the cliff top, and wrap around a bare waist, the suckers getting intimate with my flesh without even buying me a drink first.

Again, the situation might not have been too bad had I not let Lucinda borrow my Hell sword to play limbo with David.

It was out of reach, just like I was out of reach of Auric as the tentacle that gripped me rose into the air, bringing me with it.

"Kill it," I yelled as I thumped against the rubbery flesh with a closed fist.

"I'm trying," Auric snarled as he darted to the side and lopped off another limb. And it was then I noted something disturbing. Not only did the severed stump immediately grow back, but the piece that fell off? It became a new mini monster on wiggly squid legs.

"Don't cut it!" I warned, a second too late. *Thump. Slurp. Pop.* A new monster was born.

That made three little squid things whipping around and one giant mommy squid. Or was it a kraken? I never could tell them apart.

Even without my warning, Auric finally noted what his sword work accomplished, and he uttered a truly masculine, "Fuck. Now what do we do?"

Good question. With our attack options limited to punching and tiring the monster out or having a zillion of them running rampant, it seemed we were screwed. Dead meat unless we could pull a miracle out of our asses.

We needed help.

I thought it, and yet nothing happened.

Ahem. I said we were screwed. As in dire circumstances. Totally up shit creek. Fucked like a granny whose hubby took too many erectile pills.

Still, nothing happened.

I didn't get it. In the past, when I was in extreme danger, my magic always came to me. It whispered a word of power into my mind, a word that let me do incredible and deadly things.

Usually, but not today, even though I fairly shimmered with magic.

Okay, so I wouldn't employ a word of power. I still had lots of energy. I'd just have to use it. Somehow. Except…I wasn't sure how to shape it.

While I'd gotten Nefertiti to show me some cool magic tricks, I'd kept it to practical things like opening portals, blow drying my hair with a flick of my fingers, making light, tripping people from afar, useful stuff. I'd never worried about the fighting part. In the past, dire danger usually got handled by my self-preservation instinct, an instinct that was now malfunctioning.

I was broken, just like my nail that stuck in the hide of the monster when I hit it. This day was just getting worse and worse.

"Muriel!" Auric shouted my name as

the tentacle took me over the edge of the bluff.

Whoa. The dips and swerves would have been fun at an amusement park, but this ride didn't have an off button. I hammered at the tentacle around my waist, my blows doing nothing against the spongy flesh. I tossed a magical light ball toward what I thought was its eyes. The band around my waist tightened as the massive beast on the beach recoiled and heaved itself off the sandy shore, taking me with it.

The sea monster began to float out to sea. This was crazy. I had to get away. I craned my head and caught a glint of metal flying toward me along with a shouted, "Catch it!"

What had David tossed me? My hand rose and caught the Hell blade my father had given me when still a child. As my fingers curled around the familiar pommel, the flames that lived within my sword ignited, rippling along its length.

Hello, my thirsty friend.

We had a long history, my blade and me. I was a mistress who kept it well fed.

"I am going to julienne your ass!" I

screamed as I chopped down. The metal of my sword sizzled as it met the monster flesh, cauterizing the wound and, even more awesome, somehow preventing the monster from regrowing it. Even the limb that fell from my waist remained dead. So it was possible to damage the thing.

I, on the other hand, was not any freer. I'd no sooner begun to drop to the choppy waves when another tentacle rose from the sea to snag me in mid-air.

A slice and I was free again. Caught. Swipe. Falling. Snatched again. This was getting annoying. How many arms did this thing have?

I felt a flutter of wind at my back and Auric's reassuring, "I've got you, baby. Slice it again."

I swung with all my might, severing the limb clean, and with Auric holding me under my armpits, we rose only a few feet before tentacles wrapped around us again.

Seriously? I was starting to get pissed. How dare this monster interfere with my vacation? How dare it lay a slimy tentacle on the man I loved? Time to go Princess of Hell on its squishy ass.

"When I slice the tentacle holding your ankles, let go of me," I ordered.

"Never," Auric growled.

"Never say never," I taunted, and then a few things happened at once. I rammed my head back, hit my beloved in the nose, and his grip loosened as I swung my Hell blade. The suddenness of it all sent Auric shooting away from me. I, on the other hand, wanted to meet the sea monster up close and personal.

The tentacle holding me pulled me in toward the gaping mouth of what I now knew was a magical construct. Apparently, I hadn't slept through all my magic lessons. I recalled enough from my teachers to know real monsters couldn't regenerate limbs that quick nor sprout new baby versions of themselves. I could also feel the magical core at the heart of this beast.

The thing to realize with magically created constructs, golems as many called them, was at their core, there was a substance. Mud for an earth-based creature. Rocks for a stone golem. And at the heart of this sea monster? I'd wager some kind of puddle of water.

If I could reach its essence, I could destroy it. I wasn't sure exactly how yet, but I figured, by the time it swallowed me, I'd come up with a plan.

Of course, my plan might have worked better if I'd told someone about it. Instead, just as the monster went to drop me in its mouth, I heard a shout from shore.

"Harpoon away!"

What the fuck? I managed to crane my head and stare in jaw-dropped disbelief as the massive aquatic arrow came streaking at the sea monster. I didn't get a chance to see how the aim was because the tentacle let loose, dropping me into the magical beast, and I had new things to worry about, such as the fact that the insides of the thing were just as slimy and gooey as the outside.

Ugh. I tucked my knees to my chest, lest my legs get twisted during my descent, and crossed my arms over my chest, holding my sword tight. Anyone who's been ingested before can tell you it wasn't fun. Adexios had nightmares for months the first time a Styx monster tried to swallow him until his dad told him to suck it up or else he'd get him a pink ferryman robe to go with his princess panties.

Imagine my annoyance when I discovered there was no such thing as a pink version. When I was in charge of Hell, that would change, along with casual Fridays. Appearances should always be maintained.

But I had more things to worry about than banning peas permanently from Hell. Such as the monster trying to eat me getting hit by a harpoon, which penetrated its flesh and got lodged less than an inch from my ear. I figured I was allowed a little screaming along with several choice swear words. Then even more vile language as the monster lurched into motion.

Water rushed into its mouth, gallons of it, loosening my precarious perch in its throat, sending me farther into the beast.

Again, not so much fun. When I hit the thing's belly, I took a moment to express my thoughts and squealed, "Gross. Yuck. Ew." Girly moment over, I took a deep breath and called a ball of light because, within the bowels of the beast—

literally—it was pitch black.

Light didn't improve my situation, especially since I noted no amount of club soda could save my sweet bikini. Someone would pay—cash was preferred, as Auric had taken away my credit cards on account I wasn't fiscally responsible. Spoilsport.

Apart from the gross fleshy sac surrounding me, I noted only one other thing of interest, a pulse of light that faintly illuminated the stomach wall.

It didn't take my own magic reacting to know I needed to get to that light.

Since I wasn't about to trek around inside the sea monster looking for whatever was flashing, I created a direct route. My Hell blade sliced through the stomach membrane with ease, sizzling the flesh. The edges blacked and retracted, leaving me with an opening, but I missed it as the monster reacted to my surgery, lurching about.

Stumbling face-first into a mushy wall inside a monster's belly? Not recommended. The goo covering my face just heightened my irritation.

"Be afraid, be very afraid," I

muttered as I stepped through the hole I'd made into a space that pulsed. The heart of the beast and, at the center of it, a floating puddle that glowed.

It wasn't much water, maybe a gallon, two at the most, but it hung in the air, emitting a noxious blue/green glow. My magic thought I should drink it and absorb the power. Not in this lifetime.

"Bye bye, Mr. Sea Monster." I swung my weapon at the source of the construct's magic. The flames along my blade barely flickered at the liquid. A hissing steam arose, and the body surrounding me trembled. Shivered.

I zigzagged my sword Zorro style, etching an M in the suspended puddle. It was enough to shatter the spell.

The flesh tore in places as the magic holding it together unraveled. Water spilled in. Cold sea water.

Being in the belly of the beast as it sank probably wasn't a good idea. I needed out, and quickly.

A hole to my left, gushing like a broken dam, was my ticket out of this joint. I tucked my sword through the side of my bikini bottom, knowing I'd need both hands. Sucking in a deep breath, I dove through the rip, only to get caught as my sword snagged on something.

No. I didn't have time to waste. I wiggled and squirmed and shot loose— without my beloved sword. Sob. Not my precious. Yet I didn't dare return for it.

Feet fluttering, arms pulling, eyes wide open but seeing nothing, I sliced through the water, only to stop as I cleared the body.

Which way was up? Down?

I floated, suspended by the salty water. I looked for a sign, any sign of the surface or light. Yet, in every direction, only darkness beckoned. I couldn't even see the monster anymore.

I called a light, my magic not extinguished by water, but all this served to do was showcase my plight. Water everywhere I looked.

My lungs began to protest. I needed air.

Air! That was it. I blew out bubbles, recalling some vague fact that bubbles rose to the surface. Except my air bubbles appeared defective. In my wan light, I noted they hung in front of me.

Shit.

Pick a direction, any direction. I kicked and stroked, the lessons I'd taken alongside Adexios in the Styx returning to me. A child learned to flutter kick quickly when a Styx monster nibbled at the toes.

Push. Pull. Kick. The bands around my lungs tightened. My vision wavered. My motions ebbed. The last of my air escaped me.

I stopped moving, my limbs at any rate. My hair, though, wavered through the water, silky seaweed that tickled my skin as I drifted down.

And, yes, I was sinking in the direction I'd been swimming. I'd gambled wrong and lost. But I wouldn't give up. I might not have an ounce of air, but I had magic still, and I was about to die.

A word came to my lips, a guttural sound made of power, and it blew out of me on my last breath.

לעזור – *Help.*

CHAPTER NINE

The familiar sword, a dull gray without the flames bathing its length, washed ashore, without Muriel. That didn't bode well. Muriel loved that weapon. She would never relinquish it unless not given a choice.

I need to get it back to her. Auric knew her well enough to realize she'd find trouble; she always did. She'd need her weapon, but returning it to her might prove difficult since he didn't have the slightest clue where to even start looking.

"Where the fuck is she?" Auric raked a hand through his hair, staring off at the calm ocean waters, the surface deceptively smooth, not one misplaced ripple marring its glassy sheen. Not a single sign of Muriel.

"She's alive," Teivel remarked. "Her bond to me is still strong."

"I know it. I feel it, too." This didn't have the feel of his heart being torn out, not like when Lilith had dragged her into an entirely other dimension. "But for some reason, I can't follow the trail. It's as if it's shooting off in different directions."

"As if carried by the current of a sea." Teivel tucked his thumbs in the loops of his jeans as he stared at the water. "Wherever she is, it's related to that."

Auric glared at the Darkling Sea. There sat the one element he couldn't storm by force. Much as it galled him, he'd have to call for help.

The line rang only twice before it was answered with, "House of ill repute and unlawful gains. How may we screw you today?"

"Ysabel, it's—"

"Auric, I know. We do have caller ID, you know. This is not the fifteen hundreds." The acerbic reply was tossed by Lucifer's eminently qualified secretary and a true witch. As in evil spells, devil-worshipping witch who loved to block access to Lucifer with a nasty cackle. At least she used to be really nasty. Since she'd hooked up with a demon called Remy, she'd loosened up a bit. Now she sometimes only maimed those who irked her. But she still remained a very competent barrier to the big guy.

"I thought I was calling Lucifer's direct number," Auric said. As Muriel's consort, he had certain privileges when it came to accessing the Lord of the Underworld.

"You did call the big guy's private line. However, my lord has embarked on a most dangerous mission to save Hell from destruction. All hail our mighty leader."

It surprised Auric she managed to say it without snickering. "Don't tell me Lucifer has got you doing the scripted speeches again?"

"He's got some communist goof who has been assigned as his special liaison with his newest marketing firm."

The devil worked very hard to maintain his reputation. To the extent of sometimes fabricating crises. "So what supposed dangerous mission has he gone on?" Because other than Muriel's issue with the beach, things had seemed rather quiet. "This isn't another quest to discover the truly best tavern with the most buxom wenches again?" The drunken tour had made the news. The PR guys even managed to drag, from somewhere, a few demons and damned souls thanking the devil for changing their lives. Apparently, the best grog served by the most buxom wenches was of vital need to the populace.

Ysabel snickered. "No, and we also don't need to fear he'll drop his pants in public again either. He is, however, wearing a fabulous ensemble. But I won't spoil that for you. Just watch HBC's nightly news, and I'm sure they'll have a video clip."

"Where is he?"

"Sailing the Darkling Sea with Charon and a full crew. They're trying to make it in time to stop some kind of prophecy from getting fulfilled."

"Is this prophecy about a sea monster?"

While Auric couldn't see Ysabel, he could imagine her actions by the rustle of fabric as she shifted the phone at her ear.

"The prophecy doesn't specify the menace, but my understanding is the mermaids are involved."

Mermaids, after a merman supposedly coming after Muriel?

Coincidence? They didn't exist in the pit.

"Any idea how long he'll be gone? Can he be contacted?"

"Do I look like a seer?" Ysabel replied with clear disdain. "As for contact, go ahead, but if you disturb him in the middle of some kind of epic media moment, he might decapitate you. It's always good for ratings."

Lucifer and his quest for omnipotent presence. From the sounds of it, the man was dealing with an aspect of the sea problem occurring. The question was, should Auric join the devil—which even thinking it made him cringe—or did he stay here, guarding Lucinda and hoping Muriel would figure a way out?

Auric hung up with Ysabel. *I wish I knew the right thing to do.*

"We have to stay and wait, of course." The startling reply came with the slip of a little hand into his.

"Wait for what, baby girl?"

"Mommy, silly."

"Do you know where Mommy is?"

"Mommy's with the fishies."

Auric peered down at his daughter,

amazed as always at her perfection. It still boggled his mind that there were some who wanted to kill his perfect little girl. But at times like these, when she spouted the oddest things, he could see why she freaked some people out.

"Damned right she is. In a fishy's belly." Teivel never tempered his speech to Lucinda, a fact that drove Auric nuts.

"Don't be telling her stuff like that."

"Why? It's true. We all saw it happen."

Indeed they had. Auric had a bird's-eye view when the sea monster dropped Muriel into its maw then dove under the waves.

But she's not dead. "She's out there somewhere." He knew she was alive. He could feel it through the link that tethered them, and yet, that link did him no good.

"She's with my new daddy," Lucinda stated with utter assurance. "Just like the prince in my book, he saved her with a kiss."

CHAPTER TEN

The press of lips against mine might have proven more fun if they weren't trying to blow air into me.

I sputtered and flailed my hands against a very bare chest. "What the fuck? Where am I?" Unlike other moments in my life, I remembered quite clearly drowning, yet I obviously wasn't dead. So how did I go from sinking to the bottom of the Darkling Sea to making out with... "You!"

My eyes opened and beheld a familiar face. It seemed my call for help had not gone unheard. A certain merman answered it.

"Yes, it's me."

"What are you doing kissing me?" And why stop now?

He rolled his eyes, which was kind of freaky because the pupils kind of tossed like a storm-swept sea. "I wasn't kissing you. It's called mouth-to-mouth resuscitation."

"Since when does it involve tongue?" In his defense, it was my tongue that had gone wandering, but he certainly did nothing to stop it.

"I saved your life."

No, he hadn't. I'd never agree to that because then I would owe him. Debt was for fools. My dad raised me better.

I needed to turn the situation around until Tristan owed me. My gift for rational irrationality gave me the perfect attack. "You molested my mouth while I was unconscious. Total no-no, and given you're such a perv, I have to wonder, what other parts of me did you take advantage of?" And could he do it again so I could properly appreciate it? I was feeling kind of weak at the moment, and I could have used a pick-me-up. That emergency call I'd put out had taken more out of me than expected.

"I did not molest you."

"Not even a teensy tiny bit?" Why not? Did he not like a girl with curves?

"You are completely insane."

"Thank you." Our family took pride in our uniqueness.

He stood, and I noted that, once again, someone was naked, buff, and very aroused. Oh my.

"What's that?" I pointed at his erection. "Is that part of your CPR technique?" More fuel to toss on the fire—thing was the heat was grabbing at me, too.

To my amusement, a ruddy color brightened his cheeks. "It's a normal male bodily reaction to the proximity of an attractive female."

"You think I'm hot." I totally preened at the realization, thrust my chest out, gave my hair a little toss, even wet my lips.

What I should have done was sack him.

"I'd think any woman with two legs and at least one breast was hot. I haven't gotten out much since my dad brought me over from the mortal side in order to train me to take over one day."

Any woman would do? I scissored my legs, caught him around the ankles, and, with a heaving body twist, toppled him to the ground.

He scrambled to his knees, his face a

thundercloud of annoyance. "What the fuck was that for?"

"I am not *any woman*, and don't you ever forget it."

Piece stated, I sprang to my feet and took a peek around, ignoring him for the moment. I could afford to play that game because I felt the weight of his stare upon me. He couldn't look away.

Good. About time he behaved a little more normally.

I didn't choose to examine, at this time, why I cared. I certainly didn't have any intentions toward him. Nope. Not me.

Ha.

My location managed to distract me from Tristan for a moment. Where was I?

At first glance, it appeared like a cavern, a rather smallish one, the entire area surrounded by stone. And I meant entire area.

Only as I spun around for the third time did I realize there was no entrance leading from this chamber. On the far edge of the roundish space was a pool of water, no wider than ten feet across.

"Is this an undersea secret cave?" I

spun around to face him, hands on my hips.

"Of a sort."

"It could use some serious decorating."

"Excuse me?"

I winced. "Careful with the manners there. As I get older, my tolerance for them lessens." It should have scared me more that I was turning into my father, yet I'd never been happier. With sinning came pleasure. "And I said you needed some help decorating. You know, a pile of bones in the corner, maybe a few tribal-looking carvings. It's all about setting the right ambiance."

"Why would I set an ambiance that implies extreme violence and cannibalism?"

I fluttered my lashes. "Well, aren't you going to eat me?"

CHAPTER ELEVEN

Eat her? His first impulse was to say hell yeah. Instead, all Tristan could manage was a choked, "Excuse me?"

It proved fascinating to watch Muriel getting annoyed. Her dark brows drew together, her lips pursed, her eyes flashed with real flames, and smoke, literally, rose from her skin.

He'd never seen a more attractive woman. *I want her, and not just because she has two legs and a breast.*

Contrary to what he'd told her, Tristan didn't lack for eligible female companions—and even some married ones. Yet none seemed to engage him on any kind of level. None of them made him fight an urge to drag the woman in front of him close. To kiss her, for real this time. Although she wasn't wrong about his taking advantage of her. In his defense, he'd started out giving CPR, but when her soft breath rushed into him and her palms flattened on his chest, it turned into something different. Something hot, much like the embrace he'd shared with her on the beach.

"I told you I hate manners." She purred the words and took a step closer to him. Heat rolled off her skin. His cold skin warmed. He clenched his fists at his sides. She stood so close. Close enough that he could grab her.

But he wouldn't. *I don't understand or particularly enjoy this strange pull she has on me.*

Was it a spell? He needed to fight it. "I don't give a damn what you hate."

Her lips quirked. "So you're not entirely goody-two-shoes."

"What's that supposed to mean?"

"You cussed."

"I do that all the time. Big deal."

"It's the little sins that matter. But anyhow"—she waved a hand—"where are we, and how did we get here?"

"Here is one of the traveller spots that dot the path to the city. It's useful for those who need a break or to breathe. As to how you got here, I was organizing the fishing fleets—"

"I thought those were called schools."

A snort left him. "Only until they graduate. Anyhow, one minute I was giving last-minute marching orders, and the next I was sucked into some kind of mini vortex and spat out beside you. Since you were about to drown, and this cave was closer than the surface, I brought you here. A decision I admit to regretting."

He couldn't help a shiver as she ran the tip of her finger down his chest, stopping at a spot low on his belly.

"Don't lie to me. I am the devil's daughter, and I see right through you. The only regret you have is not doing this." She yanked him to her, and taken off-guard, he didn't react. Then again, would he truly have stopped her?

She commanded a kiss from him, and he allowed it. Fuck allow. He enjoyed it, the slant of her lips over his pure delight.

Her waist seemed a natural spot to park his hands. As for drawing her close, the skin-to-skin contact helped ease the tremble in him. It wasn't cold that shook him, but need.

How he needed this woman.

The devil's daughter.

The title said it all, trouble with a capital T. Yet, even knowing the drama that followed her, the exploits of her life, broadcasted for all to see on HBC, he still wanted her.

I have to have her. Such a primal emotion. It made a man want to forget his responsibilities, but a strong man never did that.

He tore his lips from hers. "I don't have time for this. I am needed back at the palace."

Once again, her eyes flashed with ire. "Are you ditching me again?"

"You are welcome to come with me, but we must leave now."

"No, thanks. I've also got better things to do, such as go home. Right now. I need to wash the stench of fish off me." She wrinkled her nose and stepped away from him. She jabbed her finger in the air and drew a rectangle. It glowed a faint red along the edges for a moment before fizzling.

She frowned and did it again. It

barely glowed for a moment, and it was gone. Her bare foot stamped the rocky floor. "Dammit. I don't have enough magic. I need a bigger kiss. Maybe a grope."

"Excuse me?"

The words left his mouth, and he didn't have time to realize his gaffe or avoid her lunge. He took the brunt of the fall, a very peeved Muriel sitting atop him.

Her slender fingers circled his wrists and held them pinned. He chose to not break her hold, just as he chose not to buck her from his chest.

She straddled him, the dampness of her bikini bottom pressing warmly on his belly. She leaned over him, the wet strands of her dark hair tickling the sides of his face.

"You are going to have to stop baiting me," she said, her brown eyes—a normal color now instead of dancing flames—boring steadily into his. "I am doing my best to resist you, and then you go and insult me with your good manners. Do you know how attractive you are when you defy me? I won't have it. I can't have it. It's one thing to kiss you because I needed some magic to open a portal, quite another to kiss you because I want to."

Part of her speech struck him. "You used me?" She'd not kissed him because she found herself attracted, but because she needed it to do magic? He felt oddly insulted. And…challenged.

"I used up all my juice getting your fish tail over to save me. I've got nothing to send me home. Unless you can open a portal?"

He shook his head. His magic lay in other areas.

"Okay then, we'll just have to make out until I charge my battery enough to call one myself."

"Or we could go the palace and have my father send you home. That doesn't involve any kind of kissing or touching that neither of us wants."

Could she hear that great big lie? And was it him or did she look as disappointed as he felt at his logical solution?

"Guess we should get moving then, although I do have a question." She stared pointedly at the puddle on the floor. "How are we getting there?"

He grinned. "Princess, I am going to blow you."

CHAPTER TWELVE

Tristan's idea of blowing and mine were completely different. His involved exhaling into a magical version of a balloon that he used to encase me. It held some of the air in the room, and so long as we didn't have too far to go, I'd survive.

It didn't mean I didn't tense when that opaque bubble floated to the top of the water hole. It hit the surface and sank a little. I stared down, but noted with relief that the water stuck to the outside. Also outside was Tristan.

What a strange enigma, that man. I could tell he wanted me. He couldn't exactly hide it, yet he kept denying it and even trying to avoid it. Why?

Perhaps he has a girlfriend. Jealousy reared its head and bared teeth. The idea of him having someone did not please me. I might have no claim on him, but my emotions seemed very determined that no one else would either.

Deal with it later. I didn't have time to worry about his possible messy breakup— because I should note blood did not come out of everything, contrary to what many websites claim. I had more important things to occupy me, such as the sudden recollection of physics and pressure and the fact that just the thin membrane of a magical bubble was all that separated me from a gazillion gallons of ocean water wanting to crush and drown me.

I might have hyperventilated for a second in panic, and then I was breathing hard because I thought I saw a merman.

Yup, I did. I did see a merman. And, wow, was he hot.

While I didn't have enough magic to create a light, I didn't need to because Tristan carried a trident made of pure energy. The white power glowed and illuminated his intriguing physique.

I'd already become fairly well acquainted with his muscled upper half, but this was the first time I truly saw him with his tail. It wasn't green or mottled. Rather he was silver scaled, from right about where his belly button was missing down his legs, except those legs were now a tail, right to the forked fins on the tip.

The iridescent sheen on his lower half sparkled as he undulated in the water. His whole body moved in a wavelike motion that proved rather fascinating. My curiosity also wondered where his great big willy went when he was in his merman shape because it certainly wasn't hanging out for little fishies to nibble on.

He pointed his trident, and my bubble lurched after him, gliding along behind as if pulled.

"How far are we?" I spoke the words aloud and wondered if he'd hear.

Since Tristan didn't turn his head, I guessed not, leaving me to just glance at the passing scenery. Hold on a second, I could see! Phosphorescent lichen clung to the perforated rocks, illuminating a façade speckled with dark openings. Every so often, a fishy denizen would dart out, ranging from mouse to hellhound size, so nothing too daunting, but there was one oceanic monster that passed overhead, casting a large shadow, that could have eaten me in a single bite.

The colorful coral reef wasn't the only thing to admire. I began to notice signs of handiwork in the form of carved colonnades. The remnants of a cobbled path meandered along the ocean floor. Bubbles, seemingly permanent ones, and much bigger than mine, dotted the landscape. Nestled within them were houses that reminded me of the Flintstones cartoon ones with stone monoliths laid in a square with a slab for a roof.

There were dozens of them, a mini village underwater. What a time to not have a phone to take pictures. It was really cute—if I ignored the icky sand all around.

The thickest cluster of bubble habitats and civilization nestled at the foot of a giant wall of stone. Slick and smooth, the rocky mountain showed only a single opening, and it was there the largest crowd of mini bubbles, like mine, and more aquatic creatures clustered.

Tristan didn't slow, nor did he feel an urge to stand in line. Rank had privilege, and he used it, something I totally approved of. Given I was here with a prince, as his companion—even if reluctantly—I was noticed. With so many eyes, and stalks, that turned my way, I posed, adopting my most aloof air. As a princess representative of Hell, I had an image to maintain, an image that was currently filthy, yet that didn't stop me from basking in the curiosity around me.

The princess awes the oceanic masses.

I could see the headline now.

The guards at the gates, barnacle-covered thick metal, were oversized crabs with razor-sharp pincers. They stood aside and clacked as Tristan wiggled through the open archway, dragging my bubble in his wake.

Within, I truly got to glimpse my first wonder, and I might have gaped in awe. It took a lot to impress me. I was raised in a castle after all, but where my father strove for foreboding and intimidating, Neptune's kingdom went for fantasy.

Gone was the darkness of outside. Within, the polished rock walls gleamed opalescent. Carved archways led off to the sides. Most of those sporting tails and gills used those passages. As for us, we headed for the golden stairs at the far end that reached up out of sight. If I craned, I could just see the blur of water distorting whatever lay beyond.

As Tristan wiggled his sweet tail to those steps, I flicked my hair, rubbed my tongue over my teeth, and readied myself. When the bubble rose high enough to emerge into air, it burst. But I was ready.

I didn't miss a step as I went from nothingness to a marble floor, the stone cool on my bare toes. Rapid movement out of the corner of my eye would usually have me leaping to action—it was always best to be faster than assassins. However, in this instance, I didn't move because Tristan didn't move.

If whatever approached didn't scare him, then no way would I react. I still had the oddest belief that Tristan didn't mean me harm. And if I was wrong, I'd kill him.

I wasn't one to forgive easily. Just ask my mother.

A warm cloak of the softest fabric was draped around my shoulders. My fingers rolled the material, admiring the smoothness of it and the pure white. What a shame it covered so much of me. Tristan sported a similar robe, but his enjoyed a rich purple hue that contrasted quite nicely with his platinum hair.

Flip-flops made of some spongy substance were slipped onto my feet and the sea prince's. Someone handed him a pair of chopsticks, and another idiot handed me a pair as well. Did they not realize how deadly those could prove in my grasp?

In this case, they weren't meant as weapons but rather as hair ties, which Tristan displayed with an adeptness that showed practice.

I snorted. "Did you just seriously pull off a manbun with no mirror?"

No need for him to reply when I could see the result. Indeed, my merman had twisted the long, wet length of his fine hair, wound it atop his head, and weaved the chopsticks through it.

He should have looked like an idiot. Alas, according to the heat between my thighs, he didn't.

Much as I hated to copy him, I emulated his movements, as wet hair really did suck when it dripped down your back, and I wanted the chopsticks handy in case my bare hands weren't enough.

At a time like this, surrounded by unknowns, I truly wished I had my sword. I could have used its reassuring weight in my hand.

Instead, I got Tristan's fingers laced in mine, tugging me. "Let's go."

"Go where? Where are we?"

"Welcome to Atlantis."

CHAPTER THIRTEEN

Some guys took a girl on a first date to a nice restaurant. Mine took me to a city that wasn't supposed to exist. Or, at least, no one had ever told me it did. Mental note to self—kill my history and geography teachers for not properly educating me.

"My dad never told me Neptune lived in Atlantis."

"Your dad doesn't know everything," was Tristan's reply.

That would piss daddy dear off. Then again, hold on a second. I knew something my father didn't. This date was getting better all the time. And, yes, in my mind, this was now a date. Why else would he be holding my hand—and dragging me along?

Despite our brisk walk, I managed to take note of our environment. It seemed historians got some things right about Atlantis, such as its name, but everything else? Mostly wrong.

First of all, the city itself resided at

the bottom of the ocean within a mountain of black diamond harder than any known rock. Within that almost impenetrable mass existed an air pocket for surface breathers with ample vegetation to recycle it and keep it fresh. Strange, but not too strange so far until I discovered that, while three quarters of the city was in Hell, in the Darkling Sea as a matter of fact, there was a portion of it residing on the mortal plane.

Or so Tristan explained as he quick-marched me along streets paved in seashells, past buildings built of pastel-colored corals.

The road to the palace, a multi-tiered architectural feat glistening ahead, wasn't exactly crowded with throngs of beings, but it was far from empty. Of interest, I noted, most of those scurrying did not appear human. As a matter of fact, Tristan and I stuck out like a horn on a horse. And, no, I wasn't referring to the false image people had of fluffy, pure unicorns. The ones I'd met with the spiral impediment were psychotic, foaming-at-the-mouth killing machines. Those warped creatures never did like me and the feeling was mutual. One day I'd hunt down that last so-called unicorn and feed it sugar cubes and subliminal messages until it adored me.

What, wait, you didn't think I was going to kill it? Screw that. I wanted one. With it as my steed, I'd trample my enemies and strike fear in their hearts—or bowels. With demons, things didn't always work the same.

As my mind wandered, I wondered if we'd ever get to the damned palace.

"Is there not a quicker way to get there?" I asked. The flip-flops I wore, while cute, did not do much to protect my feet from the pretty seashell path.

"Is the little princess tired of walking?" Tristan taunted.

"Is the little princess going to make you cry in front of her subjects?"

He stiffened then laughed. "You have a mouth on you."

"A very agile mouth good for all kinds of things." He could take that whichever way he liked. A pity his robe hid that direction.

He choked, coughed, and did his best

to keep his gaze away from me. "So, right now, we're in the eastern part of Atlantis, the Hell side."

"Is that tunnel we came through the only way in?" When in unknown territory, gather as much information as possible.

"The east, west, and north faces have access. In the southern section, which is where you'll find the Earth side, they've sectioned it off with the only portal in and out of there heavily screened. We don't need any stray mortals wandering in by accident."

"Because that happens so often I'm sure."

"More often than you'd think since humans began scuba diving. Anyone who strays into Earth-side Atlantis is heavily questioned. Only those with links to Hell can pass. I had a hard time trying to convince them I belonged."

"Did you punish them for their temerity?"

"In their defense, they didn't know who I was. I'd just found out myself."

I frowned at him. "What do you mean you didn't know?"

"I never knew because I was raised on the mortal plane instead of here with my true father."

"You didn't grow up in Hell?" That would certainly explain why we'd never met.

Tristan shook his head. "I never even knew Hell actually existed until a few years ago. I was an atheist in my other life."

Nothing could have stopped my snicker. "You didn't believe in Heaven or Hell?"

"I also didn't believe in gods or other weird shit either."

"How does that happen? I mean, you're a merman. How could you be so oblivious?"

He shrugged. "I didn't even know about my merman side and other abilities until my mid-twenties. I grew up in Nebraska. On a farm, I might add. Not much sea there. My parents never even put me in swim lessons when I was growing up."

Despite my determination to ignore Tristan, his story intrigued me. "So the son of a sea god never learned to swim. That is seriously fucked up. Who adopted you and why? Why didn't Neptune keep you?"

"The Goldsteins found me and raised me as their son. As to why Neptune didn't raise me, blame my mom for that. Whoever she was, she never told my dad she was pregnant with me. Maybe she was embarrassed she had a child out of wedlock."

"You're a bastard."

He frowned. "No need to be rude about it."

"Oh, don't be so stuffy. I'm a bastard, too. Lots of us are. As a matter of fact, on the latest census, bastards took the lead at fifty-one percent of our population. It's the newest hot trend in parenting." And I liked to think I'd started it with the birth of my daughter by not one but two men out of wedlock.

"Yeah, well, I never realized I was adopted. I might have never found out if I'd not gone on a Caribbean vacation. I took a few steps into the ocean and turned into a merman. Almost died, too, because I didn't know how to swim, and sank. Lucky for me some dolphins found me and took me to the surface."

"You're lucky you didn't drown."

He shrugged. "Not so much luck as gills." He patted his neck, and I noted the thin slits in the skin.

"So what did you do after you found out you were a merman?"

"First, I had to explain why I didn't drown to the friends I was vacationing with and the authorities. They'd all seen me go under and not come back up."

"They didn't see you change?"

He shook his head. "Not that they'd admit. Given the amount of drinking going on, they probably thought they were mistaken. Once I convinced them that the tide washed me ashore farther down the beach, I called my parents and asked them if we had any family history when it came to the ocean."

"And?" I leaned forward, fascinated by his tale.

"And that's when they finally confessed that they'd found me on a beach, nestled in a large clamshell with a blanket, a large sum of money, and a note. The message said I was theirs to keep, but I needed to be kept away from salt water at all costs. Of course, I didn't know this at the time. My parents claimed I should stay away from the ocean because of my allergy to seawater."

"But you ignored the warning."

"Yeah, because I didn't believe it. And so off to the beach I went."

"A day at the beach doesn't explain how you got from the mortal realm to here, though, and how did you discover you were Neptune's son?"

"The dolphins I'd met during my first swim apparently have cousins on this side, and they communicate back and forth. At the time, they didn't know who I was, but there was speculation. I was kidnapped from my bed at the resort the next night and taken for a swim to Atlantis. Once we convinced the guards I belonged, I finally got to meet my real dad."

"How did that go?" I recalled only too clearly my first encounter with my mother. There were times I wish the knife I'd thrown at her hadn't missed. We were still ironing out kinks in our relationship.

"It went great actually. Turns out

he'd always wanted a son, or even a daughter, but because of some prophecy, he'd abstained."

"What prophecy?"

"Some nonsense about a child of his being used to bring back the biggest menace known to ocean kind."

I narrowed my gaze. "Are you going to bring on the apocalypse?"

"No."

"Why not? This place could use a little action. Ever since we vanquished Lilith, things have been too quiet. A girl needs a bit of action to liven things up."

A moue of distaste twisted his lips. "I've already got enough dealing with all the things Neptune keeps dumping on me. I never knew being a leader had so much bureaucratic work."

"Yeah, my daddy bitches about that all the time. It's why he's got so many departments funneling stuff. Only the truly determined make it to him. It's great for weeding out the not so serious."

"Maybe I should visit and see if I could get some pointers."

"Visit my dad? On purpose?" I gaped

at him. Only fools or those damned ever expressed an actual desire to meet my father. "How can you not have met my dad?"

"Our paths never coincided. Mostly because I don't leave here often and the devil doesn't visit. Apparently, we don't have enough barmaids for him to pinch."

"So you live here all the time?"

"Yup. In the palace." Which was finally close enough for me to note it towered high overhead and sported fluted minarets as well as fluttering pennants.

"What's it made of, like seashells and coral?" I said this jokingly, but Tristan looked anything but amused.

"I don't see why that's funny. It's no worse than using rock or wood to build. It's actually rather pretty."

"I'll take your word for it."

"Actually, you'll get to see it since that's where my dad is and your chance to get a ride back through a portal."

Leave? But I'd just arrived in this fascinating place. However, exploration would have to wait for another time. My men and daughter were probably worried sick about me.

"So you were saying earlier you were dealing with some problems? What's wrong, someone pee in the seawater? Did another oil tanker spill?"

"I wish. Those are tasks we can handle. Our problem is with the mermaids. We think they've found a way to fulfill the prophecy."

I frowned. "Don't they need you to do that?"

"That was what we were led to believe. Yet, according to sources, the mermaids have gathered. Our seer says it's happening. Today. Which is why we need to move faster. I have to find out what the situation is."

"You know there's this handy little invention called a hellphone to keep in touch." I angled my fingers at my ear and mouth to mime a handset.

"They don't work down here. Too much salt in the air. It corrodes the workings. Our engineers have been working on shrinking our conchs."

"Shrinking your cocks?" What an appalling concept.

"Conchs," he enunciated with an emphasis on the N. "Spiral seashells with the ability to transfer sounds over a distance. However, we haven't been able to make them small enough to comfortably carry."

I shook my head. "And I thought I'd heard it all. That is just wacked."

"This coming from the woman who has now called me into her presence twice and yet wants me to go away each time."

"Because I don't want you."

"Then stop calling me."

"I'm not doing it on purpose." At least, I didn't think I was. "So what are you going to do with those mermaids?"

"Depends on what they're up to."

Sounded like a battle in the making. What fun. Perhaps I could delay my departure a little bit. After all, as a princess of Hell and representative of my father, it was my duty to ensure all the denizens of Hell were safe from the machinations of the truly wicked—which was anybody who actively worked against dad, or me.

I stumbled over an uneven shell, my foot turning sideways, enough that the sharp edge of the shell caught my skin and drew a bead of blood. "Ow." I hopped on one foot and glared at the offending pavement.

Then I was staring at the bristled underside of a jaw. Nice view. Before I could think twice, I nibbled it. I blamed my hungry magic for it. Never mind the fact that I totally enjoyed it.

Tristan enjoyed it, too, even if he did protest too much. "Don't do that."

"Do what?" Nip and tug.

"Suck on me like that."

"That's not sucking. This is." It didn't take much to leave a bright red hickey on his neck. My magic approved and thought I should leave a hickey farther south, but I restrained myself. Even I had limits. My men might understand a little flirty touching, but anything hardcore might make them raise a brow. Or bring down a hand.

Hmm. I was really going to have to get them to change their mode of punishment because it wasn't a deterrent.

"Did you just mark me?" He stopped dead in the road.

"Yes." In this case, the truth was allowed, as it would cause more mayhem than lying.

"You can't do that."

"I did."

"But you shouldn't have," he sputtered. "It's not right. You're committed elsewhere."

"And you're not."

"I am not going to let you play games with me. Nor am I going to get caught in some jealous triangle with your lovers."

"Actually it's more of a square."

"Stop confusing the point. I will not be another body for your harem."

Rejection again? It didn't sit well. "Why not? You're attracted to me."

"You are the devil's daughter. I have my fins full enough with the drama that comes with being Neptune's son. I don't need the added chaos of dealing with you."

We'll see about that.

CHAPTER FOURTEEN

I should dump her and dive into the nearest canal. Perhaps if he escaped her presence, then Tristan's tumultuous emotions would calm the fuck down.

The strong feelings plaguing him in regards to her were getting out of hand. The woman was involved with three other guys. She had a kid! Yet she teased him, hinted that perhaps he should become her fourth. A part of him wanted to shout yes.

No. No. And no.

He didn't believe in a polygamous relationship. He wasn't a guy who shared his girlfriends. Yet, Muriel wasn't like anyone he'd ever met. Not even close. She drew him on so many levels, the erotic one being only a fraction of it.

He found her attractive. Outspoken. Intriguing. And he had enough magic within to recognize the power within her. But it was more than that. He felt an instant connection. A sense of recognition that seemed to indicate she was the one.

But damn did she come with lots of baggage.

All these thoughts and more went through his head as he carried her into the palace that, even in the few years since he'd first arrived, never failed to impress him with its delicate beauty. A fragile splendor that trembled as an explosion shook it. He clutched Muriel tighter as he braced his sea legs on the rolling floor.

"What's happening?" he shouted to a squadron of guards who came trotting for the entrance.

"We're under attack, my lord," announced the amphibian captain of the guard.

Boom! A great rumble shook the palace, and there was a tinkle, as of glass, as shards of shell fell from above and shattered on the harder marble floor.

"Who is it? Where is my father?" As Tristan barked questions, he set a squirming Muriel to her feet.

He grasped her hand and pulled her with him, for some reason unwilling to let her out of his sight as he sought out his father.

The throne room had not suffered the explosions gracefully. Some of the fluted columns had cracked and fallen. A few had landed on the courtiers who always hung around waiting for the newest undersea scandal.

His father was pacing in front of his throne, his face florid with agitation as he yelled. "What do you mean the Undines breached the mountain? I have guards to prevent those traitors from coming near the palace."

Sir Mackeral, a being more fish than anything, even with his two stubby legs, flapped his fins. "The mermaids must have sent them, my king. The Undines only obey their command. I have rallied our troops. They will soon rout the interlopers."

"Of course we'll beat them back. But I want more than that. I want to punish those with the nerve to attack in the first place. I know the mermaids are behind this. And I also know we'll be feasting on their ribs tonight."

"But the better question," Tristan

said, "is why they did this. Why now? Is this part of the prophecy or a distraction?"

"The mermaids have found Jenny," Neptune announced.

"Who's Jenny?" Tristan asked.

"The girl who is going to open a rift and let something bad through if we don't get to her in time," grumbled Neptune. "The bloody mermaids and then those damned sirens hid her presence from me. "

"But who is she?"

Neptune stroked his beard. "Remember how I said you were an only child? Turns out I was wrong. Again. You have a sister, son."

"A sister?"

"One with a killer voice, and I mean that quite literally. She's got a deadly musical talent, one imbued with potent magic. If she sings like the mermaids want her to, then we're in a lot of goldfish poop."

He couldn't help a shudder. Giant koi made quite the mess. "So what do we need to do?" asked Tristan.

"Simple," Muriel interjected. "Kill her. If she's dead, then the problem is solved."

Before anyone could reply to Muriel's rather permanent solution, a commotion arose.

"My king." An excited starfish waved a conch shell. "We're just received word that a large ship has entered our waters."

"Blow the fucker up!" Neptune slammed the end of his trident on the floor.

The starfish wilted. "Um, my king, is that wise? The Lord of Hell and his admiral are on board."

"Lucifer and Charon are here?" Muriel pushed past him and confronted Tristan's father. "I need to get back to them right now."

For a moment, Neptune gaped at Muriel. "How did you get here?"

"He brought me." She jabbed a finger in Tristan's direction. "But I need out, and apparently you're the only one who can do it. Draw me a portal or something, would you?"

Neptune shook his head. "No can do. The mountain is in lockdown mode. No portals in or out."

"But I have to get to that ship."

Another explosion shivered the place. Neptune's brows drew together even tighter. "I don't have time to ferry you, Muriel. I have a palace and city to defend. Tristan, park Muriel somewhere safe then get your ass to the surface and see what's up with Lucifer. He's here for a reason, and it better not be to say I told you so."

"Told you what?"

Boom!

More dust and shards fell from the ceiling.

Tristan's father turned even redder with anger. "I don't have time for this. Take the princess and go."

When Muriel wouldn't budge, and began insisting that Neptune obey her, Tristan tossed her over a shoulder and carried her off with him.

She pounded on his back, which served to loosen the taut muscles in it.

"Put me down, you large, delicious brute."

"Are you going to act like a lady if I do?"

A stream of giggles was her answer.

So he kept going with her, but not to a room where he could lock her up. He already suspected nothing would keep her restrained, and since he was already going to the surface, he might as well bring her with him.

Not that he told her his plan. He let her rant and rave, quite entertained by her devious threats to his life—and manhood.

Arriving at the not often used clam chutes, he dismissed the single guard on duty with a brusque, "You're needed by the entrance to repel invaders." The chitinous soldier clacked off on several legs.

Tristan set Muriel on her feet. She stepped away from him and crossed her arms over her chest.

"You can't lock me up. I won't stay."

"I know. Which is why I brought you here."

Muriel eyed the giant closed shells with narrowed eyes. "You're going to feed me to a clam? That's new. Most guys would be looking for ways to eat my clam."

He grimaced. "That was really not the most attractive reference I've heard for that act."

"It wasn't meant to be." She smirked. "But if it's any consolation, it is delicious. Especially if slurped right."

He wouldn't think about licking that pink flesh between her thighs and sucking on the hidden pearl. But he would definitely get an erection apparently. Good thing for the robe.

Or not. It didn't seem to stop her from unerringly knowing where his cock stood at attention as she stepped close to him and grasped it through the thin material. Her lips rose and hovered only a hairsbreadth from his.

"I need to get to that ship. And if your dad won't help me, then you will."

He almost said how, except her grip tightened and her lips meshed with his. Fire lit all of his nerve endings at once. Heat flushed his skin, and captured by her sensual spell, he couldn't move away. Didn't want to.

Instead, his arm wrapped around her and tugged her close to his body, the flimsy fabric of the robes a silky deterrent. An annoying barrier.

As he tugged the robe from her

shoulders, letting it spill to the floor, so did she disrobe him, leaving him naked but her clad in the ragged bikini.

"We really shouldn't be doing this right now. I am needed elsewhere," he said in a protest that sounded feeble even to him.

"You're needed all right, here and now. By me," she growled against his mouth before nipping his lower lip.

She pushed at him, stronger than she looked, until his back pressed against the wall. Her lips devoured his, and her tongue slid along his in a sensual path of decadence. Her hand tugged at him, pulled at his cock, sliding back and forth along his erect shaft.

She controlled him in that moment, had him pumping his hips in time to her fisting. But Tristan wasn't a puppet. She wasn't the only one who could command.

Time she realized that. His hand slid down the curve of her waist to her rounded buttock. He cupped the full size, enjoying the weight, and briefly thought of grabbing them both, raising her, and impaling her on his cock. But that would mean her winning.

His fingers trailed from her perfect ass to her thighs then between them. He cupped her mound, feeling the hot heat pulsing from her sex.

A tremble went through her, a soft gasp. Moisture wet his fingers. She might be using him to fuel her magic, but she wasn't untouched. She was just as aroused as him.

The knowledge made him bolder. He slid a finger between her damp nether lips, feeling her flesh pulse around it as he pushed it in. Her hips thrust. He slid in a second finger. She tightened her channel around him. He shoved in a third to stretch her, and her grip on his shaft became almost painful.

Together, they began to move, hips thrusting, hands twisting and pulling and rubbing. The air around them grew static, magic hummed, the smell of sex permeated the air, and his body burned with liquid desire.

Their breaths came in pants, faster and faster, trying to keep up with the rapid pumping of his fingers in her sex and her hand on his cock.

He couldn't say who initiated it or how it happened. Yet they found themselves on the floor, her head bobbing over his cock, her sweet mouth inhaling him while his lips sucked at the swollen pearl of her clit, her flavorful honey ambrosia to his taste buds.

When her climax hit, a shudder went through her then another, and he jabbed his tongue into her sex to catch the wild waves. Her hard suction at his cock drew his own orgasm, and he shot his salty seed into her willing mouth, his hips arching from the floor to drive deep into her throat.

It was the most intense experience ever, and in the aftermath, he could feel the magic that coursed between them. A magic that tethered. A magic that made her almost glow as she scrambled to her feet, her body flushed and beautiful.

I want her. Not just now but forever.

He lay there stunned. Possibly in love. Definitely terrified. Because, in that moment, he realized that no amount of fighting or arguing would work. He belonged to her.

CHAPTER FIFTEEN

Dammit all to Hell and back. Despite my attempt to use Tristan only to power my magical batteries, I'd still managed to bind us together.

The thing was I couldn't seem to find an ounce of remorse in me. No matter how much I denied I'd wanted Tristan from the first moment we'd met.

I also suffered from chagrin at the realization that I'd have to explain to Auric and the others that our family had grown. Annoyance also suffused me, given Tristan looked somewhat horrified at what had just happened. Smug satisfaction also coursed through my body because now Tristan belonged to me. And finally, I felt irritation as I realized that, even though I had refilled part of my magical battery, Neptune wasn't kidding when he said portals weren't happening during the lockdown of Atlantis.

I stomped my foot. "Dammit. Who

does a girl need to blow to get out of here?"

"You already blew the right prince," was his saucy reply. "And if you'd bothered to listen before instead of mauling me—"

"Mauling? I like that word. It sounds so ferocious." I growled and swiped at him.

He didn't step back, but his eyes did smolder with interest, and was it me or did a certain part of him twitch, too?

"The reason I brought you here—"

"To have your wicked, debauched way."

"—was so we could use the clam to get you to the surface. See those holes behind them in the wall? Those are chutes, much like torpedo ones, used to get them to the surface fast."

"Why can't you just bubble me?"

"Because if there's too much agitation in the water, it could burst, and to rise rapidly in one of those means pressurization issues. The clam is your best bet."

"How do I know you're telling the truth and not trying to trick me into getting into one of those while you swim off into battle and steal all the glory?"

"You're the devil's daughter. You know I'm not lying."

The truth oozed from him like a sickly miasma. But that didn't mean I let him off the hook. "Then you won't mind a little test then. Do you like me?"

"Yes." How interesting; he didn't even grit his teeth when he said it.

"Do you want me?"

"Yes."

More truth. "So when can I expect you to move in?" Because that was the next step.

"Never."

Truth? I glared. "What do you mean never? We are tied together, you and I."

"For now."

I would have said forever because I didn't do one-night fucks, but another explosion shook the place. Chunks of rock rattled from the ceiling.

"Get in the clam, quick." Tristan slammed a fist on the closest one, and it sprang open, its inside pink and moist.

As I righted my bikini, I shook my head. "Hell no. I'd rather take my chances with a bubble."

"Fine. But don't come crying if it pops and you drown."

As if he'd let that happen. He could deny it all he wanted, but he was mine, and he'd do whatever he needed to keep me alive. Or so I hoped as Tristan did his thing, his lips pursing and blowing a sphere around my body.

He floated my bubble to a chute. Stepping back, he slapped a shell on the wall. I could almost feel the magical barrier that sprang into place. I wondered why for only a second before water began to fill the space around me. None got in my bubble, yet once again, that tiny iota of trepidation made me eye it with distrust.

But it was the bubble or the clam if I wanted to get to the surface.

Before I could brace myself, the bubble shot up, whipping upwards with so much force my ears felt as if they would explode. And then my bubble did break!

For a moment, I thought Tristan was right and I'd have to suffer an 'I told you so', except the luminance in the chute showed me the real reason my bubble had popped.

I was attacked. The webbed fingers swiped at me, missing my face but drawing scratches along my arm. Mouth closed and treading water, I faced my first mermaid.

An ugly bitch, too, with waving seaweed-green hair, a sickly pallor, and big eyes. But it was the jagged nails and pointed teeth that worried me most. I refused to end my first date with Tristan as shredded meat.

I yanked the chopsticks from my hair and jabbed. I shish kebob-ed her ass, but before I could pull my needles free, arms wrapped around my legs and dragged me down.

When I popped out onto the floor of the clam room, I heaved a happy breath of air.

Tristan said, "Now will you get in the clam?"

I did, and it was just as slimy as feared.

CHAPTER SIXTEEN

Making a grand entrance wasn't new for me. From an early age, I had an audience cataloguing my every move. You might have seen the result in my first autobiography, *Lucifer's Daughter*.

So I knew how to hold myself and command attention, to incite lust, to pull off the impossible, and look stylish doing it. Imagine now, if you would, the gray-ribbed upper shell of a massive clam, slowly opening, the curtain-like drip of sluicing ocean water hiding the contents.

Surprise, it was me stepping forth from a giant clamshell a la Venus. Even my dad, with all his spectacular ties, had never achieved anything so garish. Point for me.

Where I lost some of the wow factor was the fact that I stepped from the big, gooey thing without a priceless giant black pearl, and instead of a red carpet and an appreciative crowd of damned souls, I emerged onto a ship deck, that of the *S.S.*

Sushimaker to be exact, named because it sliced and diced.

I meant this quite literally. My dad's giant battle cruiser had some big freaking propellers at the back, which sliced and diced and made messy fish fries. Daddy and Charon liked the seafood thing. Personally, I preferred red meat. Fresh red meat. Tube steak to be exact.

But I mentally wandered—to a more interesting place apparently than the deck of this battle cruiser. Charon served as admiral on the boat, which even I had to admit was a marvel of invention.

As warships went, this one was pretty sweet. Strung together on a metal framework covered in sheeted steel for durability, this sucker could withstand any sea monster attack. So long as nothing tipped it.

As to what powered it, given combustion and other types of science-based engines didn't always work reliably in the pit, the crew on the *Sushimaker* doubled as oarsmen, who sang.

Row, row, row this fucking boat, to the heart of Darkling Sea, and then there came a mighty whale, who sprayed us with its seed.

The Vikings were a raunchy bunch. Yummy too. Big, blond, muscled men who stroked—and *stroked*—their massive, corded arms, pumping—yes, *pumping*—those oars, fast and steady. Back and forth and back, the stripped bare torsos gleaming with sweat, the muscles bunching and relaxing and…

I wonder if I could sneak off for a peek and hello.

Probably not right now, given the shell had opened and I was greeted by a few too many folks standing ready to do battle, daring to aim weapons at me!

A shame they were allies. It might have proven fun to remind them who could whip their ass.

Not as much fun as driving Tristan crazy.

But speaking of crazy, I could just imagine the type of insanity happening back at the villa. Poor Auric, which, in turn, meant poor David, as Auric would rampage. Teivel would coldly mock, and all because I'd disappeared in the belly of a sea monster. What I found weird, though, was apparently my guys had not panicked enough to tell my dad about my disappearance because he looked more shocked than relieved to see me.

"Well, I'll damn myself, Muriel, what in the nine fucking circles are you doing here? I thought you were on vacation with your harem of men and your daughter?"

Since my father held his hand out in an unexpected gesture of cordiality, I took it and hopped over the lips of the clamshell onto the deck.

"Yeah, well, you know how it is. My beachside holiday turned into a clusterfuck. New lover. New threat to Hell. Story of my life. So once again, I'm here to save the day and your hairy ass."

"I'll have you know I had it waxed earlier this week."

Boundaries just didn't exist with Dad. I knew this, and yet I groaned anyway. "Too much info. Anyhow—hold on a second, is that a ducky with horns on your slicker?"

Thrusting his shoulders back in pride, Lucifer offered a shining white smile as he showed off his latest fashion sensation. "Yes. Do you like it?"

"Only you could hope to carry it off," I replied. And it was true. Only my father could hope to wear a slicker sporting horned ducks and still project that majestic air that screamed, 'piss me off and I will roast your toes and eat them with some cheese and crackers'. I was more of a rib kind of girl. "And is that Gaia standing on the prow of the ship with her arms spread wide? What is she doing?" My weirdo of a mother stood face to the wind, and so tempting a great black shark to come vaulting from the waves to chew it off.

It could happen. I'd seen it in a movie. Best thriller movie ever. Everyone died. Well, except for the shark. He was, after all, the hero of the piece.

Alas, the mother I was still learning to bond with did not get chomped in half and apparently wasn't trying to be bait.

"Don't ask. Someone has watched *Titanic* one too many times. But forget about Gaia and her obsession with a certain movie. What are you doing here on my boat?"

The niceties done with, we got down to the real business of why I was here.

"We've got a problem. It seems some big, bad entity, who was locked away like eons ago, wants back into our plane of existence."

Some days I had to wonder at my life. I mean, when it wasn't a crazy do-gooder like Gabriel, or an angry biblical broad named Lilith, screwing with me, then it was a pink dragon for my daughter and a merman I couldn't seem to resist bonding with. Add in interdimensional super villain and it was a wonder I managed to get out of bed each day. But I did it because I loved it. Complained a lot, too. But most of the time, I loved having a purpose and meaning to my existence. A bit of zest and fun to brighten my days.

Who wanted the boringness of normalcy? I wasn't alone in my preference. The man who taught me to be me shared the same precept.

My dad drew in his stomach and straightened a dozen or so inches. Yeah, it was freaky the first few times he did it. After all, it was hard for people not to notice he didn't remain the same size. I loved Daddy's ability to grow because I never got too big for him to piggyback. I was still his partner every year at the hot sulfur spring annual Scalding Titties Volleyball match. You'll never guess who named it. Okay, maybe you could guess. The nutjob in front of me, and did I mention Daddy was wearing great big yellow rain boots? They totally matched that crazy, freaking slicker with the horned duckies, who I swear were watching me.

I could tell my dad's agitation at my announcement of a new enemy threatening Hell. Wisps of smoke curled from his ears, and I suddenly had an urge for bacon.

"Well, too fucking bad. Whoever it is will have to find another dimension to crash in because I'm not letting it cross over."

Except the problem was my daddy dear might not get a say in the matter. "You might not want to, but I don't know if you'll have a choice. Apparently, there's a key to unlocking the doorway between our world and whatever plane of existence this psycho power is on. The good news is we can destroy the key. It took us—"

My father honed in on my choice of

word. "Us? Us as in who?"

Dammit. I didn't have time to go into the weird new complication in my life—a complication who truly needed to start wearing clothes and a chastity belt.

What to tell my dad? Lie about Tristan, his best friend's son? I could hear the conversation now.

"Poseidon!" What my dad called Neptune when he was pissed at him. "How dare your son lay his filthy hands on my daughter?"

Neptune, "Let's go to the titty bar."

"Okay."

So my father could be bought. At least he had a price. Apparently, I didn't. I might not have had winky-to-pinky sex, but I'd done enough naughty-naughty with Tristan to bind him to me. He was mine.

All mine. Don't touch.

An irritated sigh blew past my lips. "My newest addition to the family. You'll meet him later. Anyhow, it took us a little while to figure it out, but apparently there's a chick who can cast a spell to open some mega doorway that will call this thing and let it in." They needed to find her, and quick, although, it might already be too late. Neptune seemed to believe the mermaids already had her in their slimy, cold claws.

"Who is she? We'll rip her vocal cords out before she can shout 'Boo!'" My father's eyes gleamed. I could tell what he thought. Great PR moment. I could see his thinking so clearly because it was exactly what I would do.

Perform some hands-on heroics— involving lots of blood and screaming for special effect—to save his iron-fisted dominion over Hell. Daddy's supporters would love the grand—and probably gruesome—gesture, and the HBC ratings would go wild.

If we were lucky, he'd get his wish. "According to all indications, in other words, some fish guts spread on some weird psychic's beach, she's somewhere around here. Maybe you've seen or heard of her. Name's Jenny. Apparently, she's got a killer voice."

Cue the dramatic music. It didn't take someone clearing their throat for me to realize I'd said something important. My words hung in the air, a breathless moment before the future split into a fork. Which way would we take?

I saw a shine of anticipation lighting my father's eyes, but it wasn't he who replied to me.

"Jenny is who we've come to rescue," an attractive man announced, the fervor in his tone unmistakable, the clenched fists at his side even more telling.

As the body of the lanky man straightened, I realized I knew him. It was Felipe, Ysabel's hellcat. We'd never technically met before, but I'd read the dossier, front to back, twice. Lately, I found myself reading more files than I cared to recall as I familiarized myself with Daddy's staff. I acquainted myself with people of interest. Some might speculate I trained to take someone's place. Yes and no.

I started taking more of an interest after my run-in with Lilith. It was the fact that she could get to me, and not just hurt me but try and hurt my family that stung most. It made me realize that I couldn't hide from some of the responsibilities that came with my princess position. One of those responsibilities, oddly enough, was self-preservation. By keeping myself safe, my family—cough, Auric—wouldn't act too rashly to rescue me.

As it turned out, Teivel held a canny grasp of politics and history. He taught me to think about my actions before killing something, which I still said was more expedient.

But I was trying to be a good student—teacher's pet with the outfit to play the part. And how did this relate to Felipe?

Well, it meant I recalled Teivel saying to try and not kill people considered friends or allies, as it could cause a few headaches. In this case, the math was simple. Since I liked Ysabel, I would hate to have to end her existence if she came after me when I skinned Felipe, her cat.

Yet what to do if Felipe planned to get in my way? I didn't need Venus, that bubble-headed so-called goddess of love, for me to see Felipe had a thing for this Jenny.

He cares for her. And yet, I knew that showing mercy to save Jenny just because he loved her didn't outweigh the wellbeing of billions. Jenny needed to die, and I wasn't just being altruistic about it. Anything unknown entering this plane of existence could prove a threat to my daughter. Her safety was my priority.

I shook my head. "Forget rescue. She needs to get taken out before the mermaids use her to let the big bad in." Mermaids were nothing like I'd imagined. It truly made me wonder where that whole romantic idea for that mermaid fairy tale came from. In reality, the mermaid I'd met would have lured Prince Eric, then eaten him, then regurgitated him to feed to her ravenous little tadpole babies.

Ugh. But apparently, this Jenny that Felipe seemed so fond of was not a mermaid herself. Or so I assumed since Felipe certainly didn't seem to be missing any body parts. Or did he? I stared at his crotch surreptitiously.

The fists at Felipe's sides tightened to white knuckles, and he growled. "You mean kill her? Like fuck."

What shocked me more was my dad's frown and choice. "I kind of agree with the cat here. Surely there's a better way. I've got my own prophecy, and it says she's going to help in the battle that's coming."

"A battle we can avoid if she's dead before she starts it."

As soon as I spoke the words, I knew it was the wrong thing to say. I could almost see the gears in my dad's head churning. In his eyes, I'm sure he thought I wanted to ruin his fun. Dear daddy did so love his little wars. Yet, before he could forbid me from meddling, Felipe inserted himself in front of me, defying me.

"I won't allow it." Every inch of him bristled with promised aggression.

Seriously? Did he understand who he was screwing with here?

My eyes narrowed as I fixed Felipe with a hard stare, one I'd learned from Daddy and that I'd practiced in a mirror. "Excuse me, but who in Hell are you?" I knew, but I thought it was time for a formal introduction.

"I think the better question is, who the fuck do you think you are?"

It was one thing for me to pretend ignorance at his identity, another for him to claim he didn't know mine. Except, staring at him, I realized he didn't show an ounce of recognition. More than a little indignant, I huffed. "That's it. I'm calling the PR department. As Lucifer's daughter, I demand more respect!" Perhaps I might have proven more intimidating if I'd dressed for the part. I had the right posture, head tossed back, hip angled, hand on it. However, wearing a skimpy bikini, flip-flops, and with tangled surfer hair, I knew I projected a just-rolled-in-the-sand-for-fun look rather than ass-kicking Princess of Hell.

"I don't care who your daddy is, *princess*. You're not killing Jenny."

If I didn't already have a now quad-sized harem, his cocky attitude might have proven more attractive. I usually liked an attractive man with a bit of alpha. Usually. Yet I felt not a glimmer for this attractive man. Not a single drop. If I truly wanted to analyze why, I'd say it was because I already had one shapeshifting feline bonded to me. It seemed that aspect of my magic was satisfied.

I had to wonder just how many

facets my magic possessed. In other words, how many more men would it force me to bond with?

A question for another day. Right now, I had to save Hell, and I totally would if a certain obstinate cat would get out of my way. "And who's going to stop me?" I asked with a smirk.

"I will."

Before anyone could fathom what Felipe meant, he took off running, his form morphing into his Hell kitty, sending his clothes scattering. My, what a nice pussy. Big, furry, and looking soft for the stroke.

Even the dirty innuendo did nothing to arouse me. Fascinating how my magic worked, but, again, not the issue of the moment.

Felipe escaped my reach, determined to foil my plan to kill Jenny. At this point, I had two choices. Chase after the feline who sat perched on the rail or wait and see. After all, there was only one place for him to go and that was the cold, icky water. Felipe wasn't the only one who'd prefer not to get wet. Hmm. That didn't sound right. I liked to get wet, but not salty.

No wait. I liked salty.

But Felipe didn't. He hovered on the railing, hesitating as he evaluated his choices. I noted he cocked his head, eyes focusing elsewhere, as if listening to someone. That someone being my mother, who got only half of her ventriloquism act together. She didn't even have the grace to look sheepish when I caught her mumbling to Felipe.

Whatever she said probably included the word jump, seeing as how Felipe launched himself into the swirling whirlpool forming alongside the ship.

I blinked and peeked again, but I'd seen correctly the first time. A twisting funnel had formed in the rocking sea's waves, like an inverted tornado that went down, down, down...much farther than I was comfortable with.

But so long as we didn't hop in like a certain dumb cat, we'd be fine.

Speaking of cat, though, the hairy bugger had dared to defy me and then escape. Already frustrated by a few things in my life, I let out an unladylike screech that I knew my daddy would wholeheartedly approve of. "I am so going to skin that cat and use him as a rug when I get my hands on him."

"Mind rerouting that murderous impulse to something a little more pressing?" my father asked, and I paid attention, seeing as how his eyes glowed, a bright red and orange and yellow, much like the flames that kept Hell lit.

People often claimed we were alike. I did, after all, have his eyes, a wart off the old hairy goat. Being alike meant we often clashed, like now when I snarled, "What could be more important than making sure your minions respect me?"

What surprised me was Daddy didn't immediately side with my desire to kill a minion for respect. Odd because he was usually the one egging me on and then taking me out to celebrate when I laid down my law.

Then again, the lookout shouted a damned good reason why everyone needed to focus on something other than turning a certain cat into a fur coat.

"Krakens!"

Dammit! So unfair. I'd always wanted to holler it at the top of my lungs. So I did. But I did it with much more pizzazz than the imp in the crow's nest who shivered in fear.

"Krakens," I yodeled with a bright smile. "Woo! Hoo!" I kicked off my flip-flops because I wanted to be taken seriously. "Give me a sword." I held out my hand and then sighed as no one slapped a weapon in it. There was the best reason for never leaving home without either a four-foot blade or my men. They'd have shoved something with a sharp edge at me. But this crew? They gave me a wide berth. That was one demographic my PR department could ignore for the moment. They showed proper respect.

"Doesn't anyone have a freaking sword?" I snapped.

"Would a scimitar work?"

At Tristan's voice, I turned to peek at the rail then blinked in astonishment because there, suspended on a wave, was Tristan, but Tristan in full-warrior mode. He wore a chest harness adorned with spikes. At his wrists, bracers laced with deadly bladed fins. In each hand he held a scimitar, the curved blades gleaming.

"Take one." He tossed it to me, the silvery length flying end over end in the air. I caught the pommel and curved my fingers around it. The weight was just right for my hand, the balance perfect. I jogged to the rail—and, yes, it had a slight slow-motion, Baywatch, watch-the-bouncy-boobs action going on. Tristan certainly noticed, as did the Vikings pouring onto the decks.

To a hundred, perhaps more, wolf whistles, I leaped to the rail, my toes curling around the pole for balance, my arms out by my sides. I scanned the horizon, seeing the churn of water and the wave of tentacles bursting from the waves.

"Kraken." I whispered the word with an edge of excitement. I'd never fought their likes before, but I knew a few crucial things—they were deadly, they projected a paralytic poison, and killing one was on my bucket list.

A boat was being lowered down the side, filled to the brim with Vikings, but I was sure they'd make room for me, even if they had to toss one of their own overboard. I readied to jump into the bobbing craft, but Tristan moved closer to me on his wave and shook his head.

"I have a better plan."

His lips pursed, and his throat did the oddest ripple as he blew a sound. A sound that should have rung for all to hear, but was silent. Whatever he did never managed to cut through the din of impending battle, yet I could feel it, a sonar type of speech.

Tristan dove under the waves, and while fainter, I could again feel the vibration of the sonar pitch he emitted.

From the choppy sea he surged, his single scimitar holstered by his side in favor of his gleaming triton, but more fantastical than that, hellphins rose from the waves, eight of them by my count, their rusty skin gleaming, the dark leather of their harnesses crisscrossing their bodies. Behind them, they pulled an intricately carved shell.

With a hint of a smile, Tristan tipped his glowing fork. "Your chariot, princess."

Now this was what I called riding into battle with style. How freaking awesome. I could practically bitch slap the jealousy hovering in the air as both my dad and mom gaped. I stepped on to the shell, wrapped a rein around one wrist, and held aloft my sword.

A moment like this deserved a speech, a cry to battle at the very least. "Let's kill ourselves a monster," I hollered. It belatedly occurred to me that the hellphins might take offense at my calling one of their possible cousins monsters, but then again, given how eagerly they jerked, maybe not.

I braced myself, adjusting my stance to the wild roll and soar of the chariot as it skimmed over waves, steering clear of the whirlpool as we headed for the cluster of thrashing tentacles. As the chariot zipped along, sluicing through the waves, I ducked and swung, the sharp edge of the blade slicing and almost sticking in the thick flesh. A wrench of my arm and it slid free, but I didn't like it.

So I fixed it.

אש, I whispered. *Fire*.

Flames erupted along the edge of the blade, not my usual red flames that adorned my Hell sword, but icy blue ones. Interesting. But were they effective?

The chariot swooped around, the loop sling shooting me toward the back of the kraken. But a kraken could see front or back via the suckers on their tentacles. A snakelike limb came whipping toward me, the mottled gray of its skin not even attractive enough to make into a lampshade. I slashed with my blade.

Sizzle. It sliced clean through and left a pleasant barbecue flavor in the air.

"You're slow, princess," Tristan shouted as he soared into the air alongside me, his silvery tail flashing. His triton slammed down on a tentacle, close to the body, chopping it short. "That's four for me."

This was a competition? What a cheater for not telling me before. My dad was going to love him. I would probably end up caring for him, too, but that didn't mean I wasn't going to beat him.

I wound the reins in my hand one loop tighter. Time for me to guide my sleigh. I directed my sea steeds through the winding and twisting morass of flying tentacles. I sliced here and there, seemingly at random, but I had an objective. The eye of the beast.

Wide, bloodshot, and unblinking, it proved a wonderful target when I launched myself, my blade sinking into the gelatinous orb.

We wouldn't discuss what oozed out—the waves thankfully wiped it clean—and I managed to irritate the kraken, which, in turn, meant a few Vikings that were caught in its grip got tossed into its mouth. Excellent.

Now to get a few more swallowed.

Before anyone got all in my face about me sacrificing the soldiers, let me say, suck it up. This was war. And two, the only way to kill a kraken, short of firing a torpedo at point-blank range, was from the inside.

I'd just handed victory to those who didn't get digested by the acidic juices in the stomach of the beast.

In moments, the tentacles went limp, hitting the water with a splash. But even the large waves capsizing a few of the teetering boats with men aboard couldn't dampen their enthusiastic cheer.

"Hail the daughter of Odin." Another name for my dad back in the day when he used to rampage and pillage for fun with the Norsemen. "May she be rewarded with a spot in Valhalla."

Screw a spot. I intended to run the place.

As I whipped my chariot around to attack the next sea monster, I winced as a noise unlike any I'd heard rushed from the whirlpool to my left. The shocking sound rose into the air. I could practically see the coils of the discordant notes as they hovered high in the sky and clung. I felt and saw the tear between Hell and the other dimension, a rip that widened but that I had to ignore as a tentacle tried to slap me.

I sliced it. I sliced all the wandering appendages and ignored the rift as I took care of the beasts threatening me and the *S.S. Sushimaker.*

The fight ended much too quickly. A handful of krakens didn't prove much against a horde of Vikings and me.

Tristan helped, too. A little. But the

guy—who obviously had some smarts—let me have the kill. How romantic.

With the sea free of monsters, I looked to the sky and noted the rip was wide enough to swallow a kraken whole. A hush of anticipation seemed to settle, and all sound stopped except for a final, horrible note that sent more than one imp screaming silently to jump into the sea.

As for me, I think my ears bled a little, but that was all. I could feel the soothing touch of a spell keeping the worst of the music from me. Damn my mother for doing something nice.

Pressure built into the air, and even with the spell shielding my ears, I couldn't help a wince. A few Vikings screamed, "By Odin's beard, make it stop!"

And then it did. There was a pop. A flash of blinding light. I blinked, and when I opened my eyes again, the sky was empty, the whirlpool caved in on itself, and nowhere could I see any sign of a big, bad monster. And I looked. But the waves were calm, no one was screaming, and nothing came lurching from the sea begging me to chop it into bits.

What a letdown.

With the enemy vanquished, I decided I should return to the ship and check on my parents. I worried about Daddy. He wasn't as young as he used to be. Once upon a few centuries ago, he'd have dove in with me to fight. Yet, for this battle, he'd stayed aboard.

As for my mother, I wondered if she'd gotten swallowed by a beast or perhaps tossed into the whirlpool before it disappeared. It probably wouldn't kill her, but anything that irritated her made me happy.

I unwound my hand from the reins and leaned against the side of my sea chariot, the image of casualness and with reason. Tristan swam alongside.

"You fought well," he remarked.

"I always do. Take me to the *S.S. Sushimaker*," I commanded my merman.

He rolled onto his back, long tail undulating, and tossed me a lazy grin. "What's in it for me?"

If this were a guy in my harem, I'd say sex. But Tristan wasn't in my boy band—yet. So instead he got, "A kiss."

I expected indignation, anger perhaps even at the small token, especially given what we'd shared earlier. Yet Tristan kept surprising me. "I accept."

In the blink of an eye, he'd flipped into the air and let out a silent sonar command. Well trained, the hellphins dove, dragging the chariot with them under the waves—without me in it.

Tristan had sliced out of the water, arms extended that he might scoop me before it went under. When a bare-chested man captured you, there was only one thing to do.

I plastered my lips to his for the promised kiss, a kiss that I meant to keep short and chaste. Ha, as if that would happen. Upon the first sensual slide of our lips, my tongue went for a walk, right into his mouth, and one kiss turned into two, three…

We stayed liplocked for several minutes, and might have gone on for several more if I hadn't heard an excited shout. "My dark lord, something rises from the deep."

I pried my lips from Tristan's and

leaned back, knowing my mouth was swollen and my skin hotly flushed, the image of a woman in lust.

I'd kept my part of the bargain. Now Tristan needed to keep his. "Take me back to the ship."

"As the princess wishes."

I wished for many things. Respect when my body burned wasn't one of them.

On a wave he created, Tristan rose above sea level, high enough that he could stand me on the boat's deck.

As his water perch backed from the boat, I frowned. "Aren't you coming aboard?"

"Not today. I need to check on Atlantis and see how its citizens fared."

I could have slapped myself silly when I said, "When will I see you again?"

"Missing me already?"

How could I miss something I didn't have? A question that had no answer, but I felt Tristan's absence keenly when he dove under the waves.

I might have dwelled on his ability to abandon me with such ease, even if it was for the best, if, at the moment, the waves hadn't stirred even more than was normal in one spot.

The water split over the skin of a clear bubble. From the cold sea, it floated, up, up, and over the deck until it POP-ped!

From it tumbled a girl and Felipe, who steadied both their landings.

It didn't take a genius to conclude this was the Jenny who threatened Hell. She didn't look so big and bad.

I turned away from the couple and took a moment to eye the large boat deck, partially covered in goop and swarming with singing Vikings pushing large brooms. Shirtless Vikings, I should add.

Sigh.

I just might have to get me one of those.

Funny how the idea of having more men kept insinuating itself. Worse, it was wigging me out less and less.

I noticed my dad's yellow slicker had emerged from the messy fight looking clean. I had to wonder if perhaps I should invest in rubber as a suit. A quick rinse after battle would save me dry cleaning bills.

"Muriel, my favorite daughter," my

daddy exclaimed, heading toward me.

"That's not very nice to say, considering you have like, what, a hundred others."

"Sibling rivalry is a healthy thing in any family."

"We're not just any family."

"Correct, we are Hell's premier family and, as such, must set the most wicked example."

Arguing with Dad was pointless at times, so I distracted him for the win. "I'm thinking of getting married. You know, tying the knot, maybe even in a church." An unconsecrated one, seeing as how I'd like my guests to survive. My uncle had this whole burst-into-flames thing going when evil things tried to get inside one of his worshipping spots.

"You're getting married? Stupendous." My dad beamed.

I almost choked. Since when did my daddy approve of legalizing relationships? "What happened to 'Muriel, I'm so proud you're living in sin'?"

"Well, your mother has managed to make me see the light. We're engaged."

"You're what?"

"Engaged. As in going to also get married? We should make it a double ceremony."

"No." I gasped, in more than a little shock.

"The abject look of disgust on your face is enough to tell me this is the right choice."

"Dad, you can't do this. I know she's been trying to make up to us and all, but have you forgotten everything she did? Are you sure you want to do something like that?"

"Your suspicion, while justified, is misplaced." I didn't need to smell flowers to know mommy dearest had arrived to shove her perky little nose into the conversation.

I glared at her. "I don't see what's wrong with the pair of you shacking up. Maybe in different houses. On different planes." Because just seeing my dad hug Gaia tightly to his side made me ill.

Immaculate conception. I didn't care what anyone said. No way could I, or would I, picture my parents doing it. Gross times a million.

"Put on your big-girl panties for at least a few minutes in between boyfriends and realize that your father and I care for each other and want to be there for you and Lucinda."

Look at that, not even sushi lunchtime and I was already gagging. I needed to change the subject and quick. "Who's that girl who popped out of the bubble with Felipe?" While I thought I knew, confirmation was always a good idea.

"That is Jenny, the girl you wanted to kill."

As I eyed her, I couldn't help but think it wouldn't have taken much to flatten her.

"Is there any point in ending her existence?" I asked.

"Not anymore. What's done is done," my father said ominously.

"We should go introduce ourselves," my mother said, patting her hair and smoothing her skirts.

"Indeed we should," intoned by my father in an eager voice.

Exactly what was the old devil up to now? I wasn't the only one who didn't trust his grin. Jenny inched closer to Felipe.

"Welcome aboard the *S.S. Sushimaker.* So glad you both survived." My father boomed his welcome and opened his arms wide.

In the sudden silence, we all heard the whispered, "Who is he?" from Jenny.

A snicker wasn't stopped in time. My dad heard me. Just like he heard Jenny. He took offense.

Flames flashed in his eyes, and my dad made a melodramatic grab of his chest—which wasn't where he kept his heart. Only someone with no enemies would ever risk an organ that important by toting it around.

I had enemies, but also a cocky attitude. Not to mention I still preferred to care, so I kept mine with me.

My father cared, too, in his own way, mostly about his reputation. "Kill me now! Or not. It seems it's not just my daughter who needs the PR department to step up their game or face eternal torture. I am the one and only mighty dark lord, king of the underworld, the punisher of sins, the—"

"Oh, can it," muttered my mom. "That's Lucifer, and I'm Mother Earth, but you may call me Gaia."

Well if everyone was going to play the nice-to-meet-you game, then I might as well join in. "And I'm—"

Jenny's eyes brightened, and her trepidation erupted into a bright smile. "Lucifer's daughter. A pleasure to meet you!"

"Hold on a second. You know Muriel, but didn't recognize me?" The revelation didn't please my dad, judging by the smoke curling from his nose.

"Uh, well, yeah. My aunts and I have been following her exploits for years. She's quite the celebrity on the isle."

I had to admit I was starting to like the girl, and it totally had to do with the hero worship in her eyes. It also meant I could totally get away with sticking out my tongue at my dad and saying, because I was the ultimate brat, "In your face. Finally someone who recognizes greatness."

I'm sure my dad might have snapped his fingers and turned me into dust on the spot if I wasn't his heir, and his favorite. Still, I smartly kept an eye on him, lest his ego talk him into killing me. I still remembered the history lessons on the Greek gods who took killing their progeny to a new level.

Apparently not everyone was wondering if my father would commit daughter-cide. Felipe apparently thought we should talk about what just happened.

"Anyone care to fill us in on what happened? I missed it when the flash of light closed the hole. Did we stop whatever was on the other side from coming through?" Felipe asked.

Judging by the exchanged glances and shrugs all around, no one quite knew.

Personally, I highly doubted something had gone through all that trouble only to fail to slip into Hell. Chances were some new menace had invaded our borders. Sweet. I'd have to make sure my sword was sharpened. Oh and find a babysitter for Lucinda in case this mommy had to take some daddies hunting.

Wee baby demon, mommy's gone a-hunting,

to find herself some evil skin to wrap her baby demon in.

In Hell, we knew the originals to all those classic nursery rhymes. It was amazing how some of them had changed to placate the bleeding hearts who abhorred violence like Jack be nimble, Jack be quick, Jack got eaten by a sea monster as he jumped over the Styx. Barely a bite, so the legend said.

From the corner of my eye, I caught an approaching mound of water and couldn't help a pitter-patter of my heart then deflation as I realized it was only Neptune. Or, as he liked to be called when at sea, Poseidon.

Soon enough I'll call him Dad.

Gulp. No. I wasn't taking Tristan in. I was not a home for lost, oversexed men. Okay, maybe I wouldn't mind having a home for oversexed men, but I already had three. And, I should add, only three holes for them to stick dicks in. No more orifices for a fourth, so acquiring Tristan, despite the bond, would be a waste.

What about giving him a hand?

Technically, I had two. Groan. Bad

enough contemplating and fighting against accepting one more man, no way would I take in two.

The mini wave spit Neptune onto the boat's deck, and he swapped his merman tail for legs—and, thankfully, a loincloth. While Neptune might appear as an attractive older man, I had no interest in seeing his sea serpent. At all. Which was good, right? It meant my magic radar might want a merman for my harem, but not just any merman would do.

Neptune's voice boomed. "Seeing as how we're all accounted for and not under attack, I'd say whatever was attempting to come over failed."

No one stole the limelight from my father. I caught the glare he tossed Neptune as he cleared his throat. "Yes, as my old salty friend here said, nothing happened. I, on the other hand, might cause some damage if I don't get some food. Anyone in the mood for sushi?"

Given the number of groans, mine being the loudest, not really.

"Something is rising on the starboard side," shouted the lookout from his post.

Good grief, what now? Had whatever jumped through the rift recovered quickly enough to attack?

Someone muttered, "Relax. It's friends, not foes."

From the roiling waves emerged a slick white sub, and I wasn't surprised to hear my dad bark, "Who the fuck owns that?"

Funny question because, knowing my dad, they wouldn't own it for long.

Jenny yelled, "Hold your fire."

More than a few people winced, and I had an urge to poke a knife in my ear, but it passed.

"Do you know who that submarine belongs to?" asked my daddy with a frown. The answer was quickly discovered, as a bevy of women emerged from it, the reclusive sirens who'd apparently raised Jenny. My dad didn't care who they were. "No fair. They have a sub? How come I don't have a sub? How am I supposed to demand and inspire respect when you women have cooler toys than me? This is so unfair."

Neptune tossed an arm around his

shoulder. "I agree, dude. But I have something they don't have. Mortal realm scotch from an English naval wreck. Care to share a glass while we discuss business affairs?"

"Shouldn't we talk about what tried to come through the rift and what we're going to do to make sure it doesn't try again?" I asked, moving toward them. "I've got a vacation to return to, and I'd like to know I can actually enjoy it without getting interrupted with a need to come to your rescue again."

Daddy snorted. "Rescue? Ha. The only thing that needs saving is me, from the machinations of your mother as she tries to drag me to the altar. I mean, whoever heard of such a thing, the devil getting married? Respectability"—he shuddered—"is something no man should ever suffer."

"What happened to let's do a double wedding?"

"Moment of insanity. Just like when I agreed to tie the knot. Oh the horror. The suffering."

I planted my hands on my hips and

glared. "The suffering? Give me a break. What about me?" I had a dilemma about a reluctant merman who didn't want to join my merry band. "What about the world?"

But Daddy and Neptune ignored me as they exposited about the horrors of marriage.

"They make you lift the toilet seat."

"Give them the biggest piece of cake."

"Expect you to give them an orgasm when you're already done."

"Sometimes they even want to cuddle."

The more my dad and Neptune bitched, the more my jaw dropped until I finally turned to my mother, who'd followed along silently. "Aren't you going to say something?"

"Say what? All those things are true. Wives do expect those and more. We like to make sure to keep our husbands on their toes."

"Speaking from experience? Just how many husbands have you had?"

Gaia smiled. "Only the one, for less than a day, but don't forget, I see everything that happens on the mortal realm. I've lived thousands of marriages vicariously through others. Why should mine and Luc's be any different?"

"Because."

"Because?" She arched a brow. "That's not an answer."

"It's all you're getting." I couldn't exactly articulate how Gaia and my dad were different. It was kind of like how I enjoyed a different relationship with my guys than most people. We were special people living extraordinary lives. The petty issues of mortals shouldn't touch us.

Yet, I'd not come on board to talk about my relationship woes or the fact that I was torn about taking on a new man or that my daughter was driving me nuts or that I was really craving a pot roast and mashed potatoes right now. Maybe then I'd get the damn seafood smell out of my nose.

I had come to stop the big bad from coming through. Since I'd failed, we needed to plan our next step, and that involved interrupting my dad's story of the girlfriend who thought he should massage her feet, for free!

"Daddy, much as we're behind you when it comes to drawing the line at touching the lowest part of a body, I think we need to move on."

"Move on where? To women demanding whole body massages? I'll tell you what they can massage—"

"Your ego," Gaia interrupted.

"My very big ego," my father retorted with an exaggerated wink.

Someone kill me now. "Oh gross. Enough with the innuendos already. It's time to get your head out of your ass, your mind out of the gutter, and focus on important matters."

"You're right, Muri. We should drink to our victory. Ale for everyone!" My daddy yelled this at the top of his lungs, and Charon, who'd glided up behind our party, scared the piss out of me when he muttered, "Oh fuck. We didn't have a chance to lock away their axes yet."

Too late. The blond goliaths already rolled large casks of ale onto the deck, and suddenly we went from heading into the bowels of the boat right back around to a barrel that someone had tapped.

The first frothing mug went to my dad, who gallantly turned around and gave it to Charon. "To the admiral of my fleet. May he get drunk and flash what's under his robe."

Getting sloshed appeared to be the plan, and that was the end of my talk with my dad. Whether he was being deliberately obtuse or pretending, it didn't matter. It seemed I was on my own to figure out what had happened and what this meant to me, er, I mean Hell.

A lovely blond giant, with braids on the sides of his head and one in his beard, offered me a sloshing tankard and a wink. I rewarded him with a flirty smile. He reached toward me and got knocked out.

The fist came out of nowhere, and when I pivoted, I noticed a familiar, glowering countenance.

Auric had arrived, and he did not look happy.

CHAPTER SEVENTEEN

"Hey, baby. How's it hanging?" Long and hard? I should be so lucky.

My consort did not speak a word, preferring instead to drag me along the deck until we reached the prow of the boat, and relative privacy.

Then he unleashed his mighty wrath—and looked mighty fine as he did it.

"Where the fuck have you been? We've been worried sick. And here you are, fighting sea monsters, by the look of it, without sending us any word."

I arched a brow. "Peeved you missed the fight?"

The tic by his eye showed his agitation. "Yes, I'm pissed. And relieved. And a whole bunch of things. Where have you been?"

I was going to answer, but wasn't given a chance because Tristan chose that moment to rise on a swell of water and announced, "She was with me."

The tic went spastic, and through our bond, I felt a quick flash of pain.

Annoyed at Tristan and his interference, I tossed the ale in my still full mug at his face. "Jerk!"

Tristan took his time slowly turning to face me, the liquid streaming down his face. He peeked his tongue between his lips for a lick—I remembered that lick and hoped Auric wouldn't notice the flush on my skin.

"What a waste of fine ale. Or were you planning to lick it off my body?" My merman appeared to have a death wish.

Auric was more than happy to indulge. *Smack.* The blow barely rocked Tristan.

He rubbed his jaw as he stared at Auric. "And you must be one of her boyfriends."

"Consort," Auric corrected.

"Jealous bastard, aren't you?"

A cold smile crossed my lover's lips. "Jealous only with dicks who seem to think they can just waltz into our family without passing any tests."

"Who says I want in?"

The challenge pricked me—and not in a naked, fun way. "We both know you do."

"I already got in. It doesn't mean I want it again."

Auric froze as Tristan's meaning penetrated. I scrambled to explain. "It's not what you think. I used all my magic escaping the beast that swallowed me. And then I didn't have enough to call a portal, so I kind of fooled around with Tristan." And bound him to me, but I wouldn't drop that bombshell yet.

But Auric wasn't dumb. "So does this mean we need a saltwater pool at the house?"

That threw Tristan for a loop. "Whoa, who said anything about me moving in? The princess and I shared a few fun moments. Nobody said that was permanent."

Auric's smile this time held a hint of mockery. "Then you should have kept your hands and other body parts to yourself. As our now mutual father-in-law would say, welcome to the family."

"Hell no." Tristan flung himself back

from the ship's prow, consternation clear in his expression.

As Auric wound his arm around my waist and tucked me close, showing me his support, I couldn't help but smirk. "See you later. Dinner's at five."

Instead of replying, Tristan dove under the waves, silver tail flashing before disappearing in the deep.

Spun in Auric's arms, I peered up at him, expecting to see more hurt that required soothing. Instead, his lips held a smile. "I'm surprised you handled that so well."

"I might have my jealous moments, but I have to look past them in order to realize that there is something at work here that is bigger than me and my urge to keep you all to myself. You have a destiny, Muriel, one that I cannot hamstring. If it requires accepting a merman into the fold, then so be it."

I frowned. "Wait a second. You're sounding really cool and logical about this, and yet you punched Tristan, and that Viking. What was up with that?"

The smile he gave me was all male—

and very sexy. "Just letting them know where they stand in the power structure. We can only have one alpha male if this is going to work. And that male is me."

Shiver. So sexy. I wound my arms around his neck and whispered, "You will always be my number one." But the one of how many?

I didn't even want to contemplate.

"What do you say we go home?"

"Yes!" I was ready to see the rest of my family. I'd missed them all.

Given I was still wobbly when it came to my powers, having expended what little I'd regained during the battle, Auric sketched a portal. In moments, we stepped onto the dry rock that comprised the yard of the seaside villa. Everything seemed so serene and surreal.

In the distance, hellgulls cawed. Waves crashed on the rocks littering the beach. Not a scream pierced the night. No raucous Vikings sang 'Ninety-nine bottles of grog on the wall'. Daddy wasn't discussing, in vivid detail, his sex life. Mother wasn't pretending everything was normal. There was just me, Auric, and a villa with a light glowing in the living room window, a light that welcomed me home.

We'd taken only a few steps onto the porch when the sliding glass door opened and a tiny body in a nightgown came hurtling at me.

"Mommy!"

I clasped my daughter tightly to me, hugging her chubby warmth. The sloppy kiss on my cheek made me smile. "Hello, baby girl. Did you miss me?"

"Tons," she exclaimed. "Where's Tristan?"

Her query threw me for a loop because I had no idea. Despite the tenuous bond between us, and Auric's assertion he was part of the family, I had my doubts. Tristan seemed aghast at the idea of leaving the sea and joining us.

But he would come around. A part of me knew he wouldn't be able to resist. Much like the sea called to certain types of men, I would call to Tristan. He would crave me. Need me. Be unable to stay away.

He'd try, I'd wager. Play hard to get. Which was fine. I did so like a challenge.

I spent a few moments with my daughter, describing the wonders of Atlantis, loving how her eyes shined. When she asked, "Can I go see it?" I replied with, "Maybe." That would depend on Tristan.

She patted my cheek. "Don't worry, Mommy. He's coming back."

The question was, when?

We spent the rest of that week at the villa. During the day, I combed the beach with my daughter seeking out fancy shells. We built incredible sandcastles and then trampled them into oblivion.

At night, after Lucinda went to bed, I made love with my three men. Arching at their touch. Panting at the pleasure. It filled me with magic. It bonded me to them closer than ever. And yet…a part of me knew something was missing. Someone was missing. I craved the cool salt of a seaman—not to be mistaken with semen, of which I received plenty.

The day came when I could delay no longer. We needed to go home. As we packed our stuff and loaded it on the deck, I stood on the edge, staring out at the sea.

This time it was Teivel who

approached me. I could tell by the cold shiver his presence wrought. "He will find you."

"I don't care if he does." I didn't want Tristan if he was too obtuse to recognize my awesomeness.

"Of course you care. It is who you are. The man is bound to you, but fighting it. It is not easy for the strong-minded to succumb to your allure."

"You didn't fight it," I stated.

I could practically feel Teivel's grin. "Because I didn't want to. I knew from the moment I saw you that I would do anything for you. He will realize it as well, and when he does, he'll come to you."

"How?" I lived in a state that didn't even border a state with access to the sea.

"Fate will show him the way."

A strange statement since I was sure my aunt didn't believe in using a GPS. Said they were the devil's work. According to my father, that was totally untrue. He threw a fit when the mortal side invented them because he did so enjoy the fallout of the old days when people relied on paper maps and got horribly lost. Nowadays, people didn't just get to their destination. They got there on time. The horror.

We left Hell and our vacation spot. Life returned to normal. I went back to the work at the bar. David and Teivel took turns helping me while Auric went looking for information on what had come through the rift. As far as anyone knew, nothing had, yet we knew something was amiss.

Days passed, days that I spent on the mortal plane, in part because I sulked. Tristan hadn't come to me. He'd not even called, and this despite the fact that I'd gotten my hands on a big old conch—the shell kind, not the big, thrusting version.

I stayed out of Hell, even when it became flooded with seawater. I wanted no reminder of the man who spurned me. But there came a day when I couldn't stay away any longer because the unthinkable happened. My father invited me to an engagement dinner for him and my mother. It was also the day a pig was born with wings.

I really didn't want to go, but Auric made me. I should add I protested quite a bit and thus found it somewhat uncomfortable to sit on my cheeks. The heated pain only served to remind me of the reward I got when I finally said yes, a pleasure they promised to repeat if I was a good girl.

Snicker. Bad girls got the spankings, so I knew what I would end up doing.

Seated amongst my lovers, dressed in a one-of-a-kind gown of red silk, strapless with high slits up both sides, I looked awesome. I didn't need a mirror to stoke my vanity. I had my men to do that for me. They stayed close to my side and glared at those who stared too long. They ran their fingers over my skin every chance they got. It usually would have been enough to have me dragging them off for a quiet corner to make out, yet I found myself distracted.

I spent most of my time staring around the vast dining hall—the stone pillars rising high in the air supporting the ribbed ceiling from which dangled massive chandeliers, the thousands of candles illuminating the room with a cozy glow. The red and black striated rock walls were covered in intricate tapestries, depicting vivid battle scenes and, in some cases, the carnal celebration ones.

Winding around the pillars and draped anywhere they could were leafy vines with bright blooms, the fragrant scent of their petals doing a fair job at masking the usual brimstone of home.

Everyone who was a someone was in attendance. Even my brother, Christopher, who had obviously objected to coming seeing as how he was tied to a chair, and gagged. He still resented finding out Lucifer was his dad, and of late, they'd been fighting even more than usual given my dad was insisting he honor some old oath that wanted him to marry Rasputin's granddaughter.

None of my business. I'd done my part to grow the family by taking on three—should have been four—and popping out a menace to society in the form of my lovely daughter, Lucinda, who played tag with the demon children in the ballroom watched over by my dad's most awesome guards and David. He was über protective when we came to the pit, not trusting the former thieves and assassins who inhabited my childhood home. That was what he claimed as he strode off with our daughter. I loved that he lied to me, especially since he knew that I knew that he preferred wearing his kitty and playing with the little ones to the pomp and ceremony of a dinner.

I wished I romped with them.

Of all the dinners I'd attended hosted by my dad, this was the most boring. Seriously yawn worthy. I expected that from my mom, I mean just look at her dress. Dressed in green, again, and covered in flowers. Boring. Dad at least tried with his red velvet suit topped off with a devil-duckied tie. I suspected he did it to drive my mom nuts. She was always trying to get my dad to dress more sedately. As if my dad would ever let her change his style.

As the reception went off without a hitch, despite the best attempts by the hired imps to trip waiters and have couples caught in flagrante delicto, I could see my dad getting more and more dejected. I got how he felt. I'd kind of hoped to see a certain someone at this shindig. I mean, Neptune was here as best man, but of his son Tristan? Not a single peek.

How was I supposed to wow him and make him grovel and beg for me to take him home with me if I couldn't even see him?

"He's here," Auric murmured in my ear as they brought out the first course.

"Who is?" Playing dumb was something my sister Bambi had taught me. Speaking of whom, why was she sitting with my other half sisters and not with Chris, Auric's mage friend, who stared at her with evident longing?

I had to wonder if she was utilizing part of her lesson plan from Playing Hard To Get, the master class. My sister was a pro when it came to getting men to do as she wanted. Perhaps it was time I went back to her school. Apparently, I needed some pointers since I'd yet to land my fish.

"Your merman is here, but he's playing coy."

"He's in the pond?" Was he flirting with the golden koi? I'd skewer them with a spear and roast them over the fiery centerpiece that my mom claimed was the reenactment of Pompeii—and that dad declared was where I was conceived. Ugh.

I'd never be able to eat molten lava chocolate cake again.

Auric sighed. "I mean coy, as in he's staying out of sight."

"Then how do you know he's here?" Because Auric had never left my side since we'd arrived. He had this thing about trusting Hell. Apparently, his former angelic habits clung, and he worried I'd get corrupted or something. So funny. If anyone needed to worry, it was him. With me. I was the biggest corrupting influence he knew. The ability to subvert came naturally to me.

"He's here. Trust me. And he's been watching."

I straightened in my seat, the better to show off my bare shoulders and daring décolletage. "So what's the plan?"

The gaze he turned my way held a puzzled frown. "A plan for what?"

"Why, capturing my fish of course. We didn't get the work started on that pool and the underground grotto for nothing." Plans, I might add, that Auric took on because I sulked about the man who'd swum away from me.

"Muriel, we are not going to force him to join us. He'll come when he's good and ready."

But I was ready now. My inner magic wasn't the only one screaming we needed Tristan. There was a hole in my force. Without Tristan, I was incomplete.

Something prickled at me. It wasn't a breeze, or a burst of magic, yet I could tell something had happened. My dad noted it, too. He sat back in his throne, a custom-designed seat carved from a solid block of obsidian and inlaid with precious gems. A matching one alongside held my mom. As for me, the best princess ever? I got only a golden chair. Bummer.

While my dad feigned inattention, I craned to see what had the crowd at the far end of the room aflutter. I could hear snatches of conversation.

"Who is that woman?"

"Are those tentacles?"

"Does she have three breasts?"

Indeed the unknown woman did. She came gliding up the cleared area left open by tables placed in a u-shape. The entertainment—sword swallowers, dancers, and other damned souls hired for the event—moved out of her way. I could see why. The woman projected presence, and three breasts encased in a tight mermaid dress that shimmered with all the colors of the sea. From under the hem, I thought I saw something slither. But I blinked, and it was gone.

Dark hair in shining, green, curly waves danced down her back, the strands almost alive much like Medusa's serpentine crown. The woman sashayed her way, head held high, an imperious tilt to her head and smile.

I disliked her on sight, especially since she drew so many eyes, including that of my consort.

I growled at Auric. "You'd better not be staring at her triple boobs."

"Do you know who that is?" he whispered back.

A dead woman if she so much as looked at any of my men.

I heard my dad groan. "Fuck me, the sea hag is back."

"The sea hag is back." The words were repeated in a chain reaction by all those

present as the woman continued her sinuous glide between the tables headed straight for my mom and dad.

I felt no remorse at eavesdropping on my parents.

"You can stop staring anytime," grumbled Gaia, and I noted her elbow drew back and jabbed Daddy in the ribs.

Not at all perturbed, my father clasped her hand in his. "And deny you the enjoyment of jealousy? Even I am not so selfish, wench."

"I am not jealous."

"Such a liar," he murmured. "I love it. I know you hate the fact I slept with her."

I blinked. My dad slept with that woman? Ugh.

"I don't believe it. That's Ursula," Teivel muttered in a low breath.

"You know her?"

"Know of her, and she is bad news," Teivel murmured against my ear. "We should be wary."

"At least you didn't marry her. What is my ex-wife doing here?" groaned Neptune before he ducked down behind the table.

Ex-wife? Holy shit. It seemed my dad's boring party was about to get more exciting. About time.

My father shifted in his seat as he grumbled. "I don't fucking know, and I don't like it. Who had the balls to invite the hag to my party?"

"I thought she was locked in another dimension after her *incident*," my mother whispered with a gesture, the coo-coo one that involved circling a finger at her temple.

"Yes, I was locked away. Cruelly and unjustly," the hag said when she reached the head table. But she didn't just stop. She posed, angling a hip and placing a hand on it. I was sure she meant to look sexy, yet there was something cold and dark in her eyes. Something that said she'd eat you— and not in a nice, slurpy kind of way.

My dad replied to her accusation. "You went off your rocker and tried to destroy the world. That kind of thing tends to get noticed."

She had? Why had I not heard of this? Exactly how many secrets did my father keep from me? If I was to take over one day, I needed to know this kind of stuff. I also wanted to know what the heck this sea hag person was planning because I could feel power pulsing from her in waves. The woman leaked energy, and for a moment, my magic stirred with interest. It could use a new foreign flavor.

Not happening. I slammed the door shut on it. Women were cute. I liked playing with titties, and a pussy, my own I should add. But when it came to intimate acts, give me a dick, or three. Or if a certain merman would stop being so stubborn, four.

"I was a tad upset after my breakup with that cheating manwhore." The woman's storm-sea eyes narrowed on Neptune, despite his attempt to cower behind the table.

The sea god finally found a pair and came out of hiding. Neptune straightened in his seat, thrust his shoulders back, and stroked his beard. "Maybe I wouldn't have had to step out if you put out more."

An "oooh" went through the room, and I was a part of it. In a sense, I could understand Neptune cheating. People had needs, but still, I knew what I'd do if my men ever stepped out on me—and, no, I didn't consider what I'd done with Tristan the same. As Auric explained as I'd sobbed in regret, "You do what you have to in order to survive." Some people had to kill. Some people had to pretend to like things. I had to have awesome sex.

My life was utterly warped, yet fun.

I think the whole room held its breath as we waited for Ursula to react.

Nothing happened, unless we counted the appearance of a tiny tic by Ursula's left eye.

"Who truly cares who's at fault?" Ursula coughed in her hand. "You." She smiled, and it had all the warmth of a shark's grin. "I am back now, and I didn't come here to rehash the past. I've had time to get over that silliness. I have a much better sex life now." Her laughter emerged high-pitched and ominous. "Today is one of celebration. The Lord of the Pit, the demon who helped lock me away in that dreary dimension, with no one to speak to but my constructs and unevolved creatures, is planning to get married. That deserves a gift."

No fair. How come my daddy got all the presents? As a princess, and heir, shouldn't she cater to my goodwill, too?

"How about returning the wilds back the way they were?"

Ah yes, the wilds, which had apparently turned into a sea. A shame because the spiders in the wild swamp used to make the strongest silk.

Ursula flung her head back and placed a hand upon her temple. "Trying to kick me out of my new home already? And after all the time and effort I spent creating it?" She snorted and tilted her head to face him. Her swirling eyes took on the color of an arctic sea, cold and uncompromising. "Not happening. I am back, bitches, and I am here to stay. And in a gesture of goodwill and a sincere wish to make things work, I want to give you the kiss of peace."

I was pretty sure I wasn't the only one disappointed by her offer. A little violence and mayhem would have really livened up the party. I'd bought new stilettos for the occasion, the tips pointed enough to puncture—for which I was in trouble for demonstrating on Teivel's motorcycle tire. Apparently, his custom wheels were expensive.

As Ursula's juicy red lips puckered for a kiss, my dad recoiled. "Couldn't we just shake?"

Was I the only one who noticed Ursula's tightening jaw? Someone was a little insulted.

"In order to make the peace between us binding, it requires something a little more *intimate.*"

I blinked and thought happy thoughts, like me beheading Azazel and his minions, lest I go blind at the very thought of my dad and Ursula doing the wild thing.

In what I think shocked more than a few of us, my mother seemed on board with Ursula's demand. My mom shoved my dad and rebuked him. "Don't be such an imp. It's just a kiss. Take it like a demon and get this over with."

"But you told me I wasn't allowed to touch anyone else. You threatened"—my dad lowered his voice, but my hearing was still good enough to hear—"my manparts if I did."

"You still aren't, except for this one case. Now pucker up, buttercup, and take your kiss like a big boy."

"Fine. But I won't like it." The grimace on Dad's face owed more than just telling the truth. He really didn't want to kiss Ursula. And that said a lot given my dad would kiss just about anything, even a pig in lipstick. I had the picture proof locked away in a safe for future blackmail.

With a look much like that of a man expected to walk himself to the gallows, my dad leaned forward and presented his mouth. Puckered like a fish. He closed his eyes, too, as Ursula pressed in close, her heaving three bosoms leaning forward and threatening the low-cut décolletage. My dad, however, didn't move in for the kiss. He held himself rigid and morose.

Not daunted by his lack of interest, Ursula angled forward just far enough that she could press her lips against my dad's. The room held its breath, and perhaps it was the stillness that let me feel the tiniest of jolts in the air.

A spell had been triggered. But where, and what?

As I scanned the room, eyeballing, in turn, the guests, I saw nothing amiss. Everyone seemed intent on what occurred at the head table.

They were probably disappointed. I knew I was. Nothing happened. No screaming or bloodshed or monster from the deep bursting through the slag and embarking on a rampaging slither through the castle, eating guests. A shame. I'd heard the stories of the reception in seven ninety-two B.C. People still sang of the mighty battle against the serpent who lived in the core of our world.

But we didn't get to scream—in delight—or draw a weapon—which, while banned from the reception, I could guarantee hid upon many a body present. I wore knives, enchanted to be invisible where they were strapped on my arm.

Nothing happened. Not even my dad tossing Ursula on the table in front of my mother and having his way with her. I'd never seen it happen, but again, according to history, daddy dear wasn't shy.

Alas, he didn't give my mother a reason to call off the wedding. He stood, a statue with a stunned look on his face.

A relieved sigh went through the room as it didn't explode into a ball of flame and the guests didn't see the floor crack open and swallow them. So boring.

I drummed my nails on the table and frowned as I noted my dad quickly scanning the room. What did he look for? Why was he suddenly smiling like an escaped mental patient with an axe and a head full of voices?

I leaned close to Auric. "Something's wrong with my dad."

"There's a lot of things wrong with him. You'll have to be more specific," was my consort's retort.

Yet Teivel must have caught some of what I did. He rose from his seat and took a step back. He did that only when he planned to leap. As he'd confided, to look cool, always leave enough room to jump. It didn't provoke the right kind of terror if you leaped and caught your foot on something and landed on your face.

I silently urged him to tackle Ursula.

But, instead, I think we all froze a little and wondered if we were about to die because my dad held out his arms wide, cracked an even wider grin on his face, showing all of his white, so very white, chomping teeth. "I love you! Each and every one of you. Group hug!"

Hug? From my dad? What had we done that he wanted to punish us? I caught Bambi's eye, and she shook her head and rolled her shoulders. I wasn't alone in wondering what the heck was going on.

Daddy wiggled his arms, beckoning with the tips of his fingers. "Come on. Don't be shy. Let's share the love."

My mother rose from her seat, her frothy gown making only the barest whisper of sound. "Um, Luc, are you feeling all right?" She placed her hand lightly on his arm.

Dad whirled, and I sucked in a breath. Was he going to finally make me a half orphan? He grasped Gaia's hand and didn't crush it. Instead, the oddest look crossed his face. "Never better, my beautiful fiancée. Have I told you how much I love you? And how excited I am that we're getting married and spending the rest of our lives together? Ooh. Do you know what would make our wedding day even better?" my father gushed.

My. Father. Gushed. Something was seriously wrong.

Even my mother noted it as she said tentatively, "What?"

"Abstaining from intimate acts until the big day."

As my mother gasped, "What?" Auric muttered, "Okay, you were right. Something is seriously wrong."

Someone was seriously broken, and I could have sobbed as I heard my father's next emasculating words.

"Think of it as me showing my respect and affection for you. My beloved." The wide smile on Dad's face should have appeared beatific. The devil's face wasn't meant for that kind of unnatural grin. He frightened me, and more than a few people gagged.

"Luc, are you screwing with me?" I could hear and see the worry in Gaia's query.

"Never, my gentle dove." Daddy clasped Gaia's hand to his chest as he uttered the most fervent, and stomach-churning, truth.

Gaia tore her hand from his grip and whirled away. I could see the shock and disbelief on her face, but only for an instant before rage tightened her features. Up popped her head, green eyes blazing with flower power—which I could admit was kind of cool. Hands braced on her hips, Gaia barked, "Get your fat ass back here, you psycho, dimension-escaping hussy. What did you do to Lucifer?"

Only as I tore my gaze from the fascinating scene unfolding between my parents did I note Ursula seemed intent on making her escape. Yet, at my mother's words, she stopped and pivoted.

Ursula clutched at her breast and widened her eyes in a look of innocence I didn't buy for a minute. "What did I do? Why only what I said I would. I gave Lucifer the gift of peace. Oh, and it might have had a smidgen of love and respect in there. Look at him. He's a changed man already." From deep within her three-boobed bosom emerged a laugh, the slow, rolling chuckle of pure evil. "Muahahaha. Muahahahaha."

Damn, I should have taken notes because she had that chuckle down to a tee.

"Change him back," my mother growled.

Ursula tapped a manicured nail against her chin, as if in thought. A smirk twisted her lips. "Um, no. Like I said, the bitch is back, and I am promising some trouble. Enjoy your pussy of a boyfriend!"

My dad, a pussy? Never.

Before anyone could tackle her ample ass, with a snap of her fingers and a poof of smoke, Ursula disappeared from sight.

"Wasn't that just lovely of her to pop in like that?" said my dad with a hundred-watt smile. "Now who wants some cake? Don't forget to say please."

I think I might have let loose a sob at that point. I do know Auric's arm came around me. He whispered, "Don't worry. We'll figure out what's wrong and fix him."

But we couldn't fix what we couldn't find. It wasn't for a lack of trying. Even Nefertiti could not detect a spell on him.

The Egyptian sorceress, in her youthful guise and wearing the sheerest, and clingiest, of togas, removed her fingers from my dad's temple. "I cannot find any traces of magic on him."

"Impossible," my mother countered. "She obviously did something. Look at him. He's freaking prince charming on goody-two-shoes steroids."

Eloquently put. As utterly gross as it sounded, my dad was now a polite and wonderful man, a boring dude just like my uncle.

"There must be a way to fix him. Maybe this is like the time Mom"—I cast her a glare— "did that spell to make everyone forget Lucinda."

Gaia rolled her eyes. "Oh, get over it already. I did it for the good of the world."

"The good of the world would be better served by you erasing pollution and not fucking with the climate."

My mother glared at me. "Now is not the time for your hippie, eco views. Your father is incapacitated."

"And has been since his decision to marry you." I sulked. Perhaps one day I'd forgive my mother. Then again, probably not.

"Whatever your feelings on our relationship, we have bigger things to worry about now. And you raised a good point about how you managed to wipe my spell. Just do it again."

I could have choked, and I would later on a cock or two if Mother had her way. The way I'd broken the spell last time had involved an orgy with three guys. Yet, would three be enough?

Why wouldn't it be? I tried to tell myself. Meanwhile, my thoughts strayed to a certain platinum-haired sea god. With four, I would be much more powerful.

Or was I being selfish? Why did I want to drag Tristan into my world so badly?

Um, because I am selfish. I wanted Tristan. As Lucifer's daughter, I would have Tristan. As a woman, I needed him.

And dammit, I really didn't give a hoot if he wasn't crazy about joining my growing harem. He would do it because the kingdom of Hell needed him to man up and put out.

"Uh oh," Teivel whispered. "She's got that look again."

I had the look and the desire to save the day. "Mom, take Dad to his bedroom. I need you to keep him out of sight." Lest his minions see him during this moment of weakness. "I'm going to try and fix this. Whatever you do, don't leave until I'm done."

And by done I meant I'd be nearby making magic with my lovers. A magic that I'd project at my dad and hopefully snap whatever spell held him.

Marathon orgy sex for the good of Hell. There were days I loved being a princess. And days I wished I were queen so I could chop off some heads without repercussion.

CHAPTER EIGHTEEN

It didn't take long for David and Teivel to track down Tristan, but while I waited with Auric, I paced.

"I shouldn't do this," I muttered. "We have a good thing going."

"We do. And it will still be a good thing tomorrow, albeit with one extra face." Auric sat in a chair, completely at ease.

"I don't want him."

"Yes, you do."

"He doesn't want me."

"Yes, he does. Or did you think tonight was the first night he spied on you?"

That stopped me. I whirled to face Auric. "What are you talking about? Tristan hasn't come to the house, and this is my first time back to Hell since our vacation."

"The man has been keeping tabs on you, or did you not notice the sudden influx of fish tanks all over the house?"

"Lucinda wanted a pet."

"Lucinda gave him a way to see you. And he took advantage."

"You allowed it?" Sometimes Auric was an enigma to me. At times, he'd rage with jealousy; at others, he was so calm and analytical I wondered if he was bipolar. Just another reason to adore him.

"Let me ask you, since you met Tristan, have you had any more urges to go to the beach? To bathe in salt water? Woken up from any strange wet dreams?"

I awoke wet a lot, but mostly because someone was fingering me awake. So much better than an alarm clock. "No, that all stopped, but I don't get what you're implying."

"They stopped because you've found the element you need to complete that part of your magic."

"Tristan is more than just an element," I retorted. He was a man, with morals and honor and…

Auric nodded as if he heard my thoughts. "He is more than that, which is why I can accept it. You don't just pick up guys because you're horny, Muriel. You attract men that help complete you, not just magically but emotionally."

"I barely know him."

"Yet you know enough to care." Auric stood from his seat and took me in his arms. "You are my life, Muriel, and that life includes other men."

"How many?" I whispered.

"As many as it takes to fulfill your destiny."

His words sent a chill through me. *What is my destiny?*

At the moment, it apparently involved convincing an unwilling merman to have an orgy with me and three other guys.

The door to the mistress bedroom was flung open as David and Teivel returned, a stormy-looking Tristan held between them.

"Tell your boy toys to let me go," Tristan spat through gritted teeth.

Boy toys? I let my anger at the insult bolster my courage. "My men are not controlled by me." Except for Teivel in the bedroom.

"We are with Muriel because we want to be. We need to be," David said, relinquishing his grip.

"It's perverted," Tristan spat.

"But fun," I added.

"And perverted only according to those following the doctrines and morals religion created." Auric entered the argument.

"So, that's something you're comfortable with. It doesn't mean everyone is. I prefer one dick in the bedroom. Mine."

I caught the lie and frowned, but Auric was the one who busted him.

"Is that why you're watching us in bed every night?"

He was?

"Is that why, even now, your heart is pumping faster?" Teivel whispered by Tristan's ear.

"I can smell his arousal," David growled, his eyes flashing with the wildness he kept caged.

"Watching is one thing. I can't be a part of this."

"Why?" I asked the question as I

walked toward him. He dropped his chin, but it took only a single fingertip to lift it. "Why are you fighting?"

He closed his eyes tight and didn't answer.

I leaned closer and whispered, "You haven't even tried it. So how can you know what you want?"

His eyes shot open and blazed with the storminess of a sea. "What if I did try and couldn't handle it? Would you let me go?"

I wanted to say no, but I had to trust—such a disgusting word—that, once he tasted the temptation, he wouldn't want to leave. "Help us make magic. Help me save my father. If, after that, you still don't want me"—not easy words to say—"then you can leave and I'll never bother you again."

The promise hung in the air, noted by the forces that kept vows in check.

For a moment, Tristan stood silent, at a crossroad of choice, one where he'd enjoy extreme pleasure with me, the other where he'd die horribly by me. I already knew I wouldn't take his rejection well.

The smart man chose to live.

"So how do we do this?"

Good question. We were in the right place at least. The room we'd borrowed was known as the mistress bedroom, as in where Daddy had kept his lady friends when I was growing up. He didn't keep them in these secret chambers to protect my sensibilities, but more to ensure his other mistresses didn't know about each other. My dad used to be the ultimate ladies' man.

Now he was monogamous, the poor guy, but maybe if I fixed him, he'd also realize that he was better off staying away from the altar.

A girl could try.

I would also have to try figuring out how a fivesome was going to work. Nefertiti offered pointers, but as I'd learned since meeting my lovers, hands-on was so much more fun and informative.

The bed beckoned while the men kind of stood there, my three older lovers on one side taunting Tristan with smirks while my merman gave them an evil fish eye.

The posturing made me roll my eyes. "Boys, behave. Tristan has decided to give us a test drive, so the least you can do is get naked." Before he changed his mind.

As to their coolness toward each other? I wouldn't ask them to be friends. A little healthy rivalry would keep them on their toes.

Since it seemed rude to ask them to strip, given I remained clothed, I took care of matters.

The lacing at the side of my gown loosened with the pull of one knot. Four sets of eyes watched me. Excellent. My hands palmed my waist and gripped the red skirt. I tugged, the fabric clinging for a moment to the erect tips of my breasts before popping loose. In moments, fabric billowed down over my hips into a silken pool at my feet. I hooked my fingers into the thong I wore, red just like my dress.

"Anyone going to join me?"

It started with Auric, the alpha leader of my men. Once he moved, they moved, too, although given his alpha tendencies, I could see Tristan balked. His jaw set. For a moment, I wondered if he'd change his mind and walk out.

I willed him to stay and threw in a little gyration of my hips to help. That cemented it. Clothes went flying, and in short order, I gazed upon four utterly delicious, naked men. *Mine. All mine.*

While they didn't speak aloud, they apparently held some plan in mind as they moved, each with his own lanky male grace. I couldn't help but feast my eyes on all of them. How had I ever gotten so lucky? While Auric would always be my first love, and soulmate, here were three more that I could say I loved, too. They belonged with me. In my bed and in my heart. They also belonged *in* me.

Before they could reach out to grab me, I pounced onto the bed and put myself in a doggy position. I peeked at them over my shoulder.

While I knew I couldn't get away with ordering Auric, David, and Tristan, there was one in the group who liked me to tell him what to do. "Teivel. Stroke yourself for me."

The command excited him. His eyes bled to black as his fist grasped his thick shaft and pumped it. How I did so love to watch, yet I wouldn't get much of a chance, given a very happy cock waved in my face.

A hand, covered in calluses and scars, stroked the hard dick. I knew that hand, and so I smiled as I peeked at Auric. "Is that for me?"

His reply was to grab me by the hair and guide my lips. Great plan. I opened my mouth wide and took him in. I let myself slide over his silken head, enjoying his length, stretching wide over his width. My tongue made its own wet mark, caressing skin as I pulled on his dick. As I pulled back, I suctioned, hard enough to hollow my cheeks. His fingers dug into my scalp as he let out a low moan. He wasn't the only one making noises.

A glance to my left showed Tristan, not as shy as feared, stroking his cock, his eyes bright. A peek to my other side and I noted Teivel still playing with his hard dick.

But where was my kitty? I didn't see David, yet I could sense him close by.

Try behind me. His hands palmed my ass cheeks. He spread me, and I quivered in anticipation. Warm breath fluttered across my pussy lips. I shuddered, and honey moistened me further.

As David blew on me, I couldn't help but bob my head on Auric's cock. Sometimes the wait for a lover's intimate touch was as exciting as the act itself.

David loved to tease. His mouth touched me, just not where I wanted. He placed feather-light kisses on my inner thighs, and every so often, he blew on my sex.

Delightfully distracting, so much so that when a mouth, make that two, one on each side, latched onto my hanging breasts, I squeaked, my teeth clamping down for a moment on Auric's cock.

Oops. He drew in a sharp breath and thrust his hips, letting the flat edge of my teeth drag along his skin. A little pain went well with pleasure.

Maintaining a rhythm proved hard, given David finally lapped at my sex, his raspy tongue dragging against my sensitive flesh. As if that weren't exciting enough, Tristan and Teivel bit and sucked at my nipples, sending jolts of pure pleasure to stimulate me further.

My head bobbed on Auric's shaft, his threaded fingers tugging me back and forth. A hum vibrated his length, as I couldn't help making noise at the intense pleasure of it all.

David worked my clit so well, his tongue, flicking rapidly across it, drawing a small climax from me, the waves of it rippling my channel. Before those tremors could subside, David moved, the bed dipping slightly just before he slammed his long cock into my moist sheath.

I cried out, the sound muffled by the shaft in my mouth. The lips working my nipples drew harder, and the men's hands touched me, rasping along my skin with delightful friction. Given my distraction, Auric took his cock away from me, the jerk, but only because he had more nefarious plans.

"Teivel, hold her hands above her head while I take a turn fucking her."

Oh, the dirty words. I almost came on David's pumping cock. My arms were pulled and the wrists locked in Teivel's cool grip. A glance showed my vampire kneeling on the bed, his cock jutting like the hardest of marble from his groin.

"Feed it to me," I ordered.

"Don't give it to her," Auric countered. "Make her look and crave."

Look but not touch? The cruelty.

Even crueler, David withdrew, but only so another could take his place. I knew this cock. Thick and hot. Auric always stretched me when he penetrated. He seesawed a few times, and I mewled and wiggled, beyond the point of bliss. Just aching for him to finish me off.

Instead, Auric slowed. "Come here, merman. I want you to see how wet she is."

I couldn't see, yet a part of me knew what happened. Auric withdrew from me but only so he could grab Tristan's hand and press it against me.

Those fingers trembled.

"Fuck her." Auric whispered the command, and David repeated it. "Give it to her."

"Give it to her hard."

For a moment, nothing happened, and I feared we'd spooked Tristan.

I cried out when his cock slammed into me.

"That's it," Auric crooned. "Fuck that sweet hole of hers. Get her nice and juicy because you're going to need that lube when you take her ass."

I'd long lost my fear of things going into that hole, but it seemed the idea was a new one for Tristan. He paused in the act of fucking me, not long, before he slapped against me, harder and deeper.

I panted and stared with longing at the cock out of my reach. It didn't help that glances to my side showed David and Auric stroking themselves, waiting for their turn.

"Switch with me," Auric commanded.

Tristan withdrew, and they swapped spots. I clawed at Teivel's thighs because that was all I could touch since he held my wrists pinned. Auric's hard thrusts rocked my body, the fat head of his cock slapping my sensitive G-spot.

The pleasure within me coiled, tightened, readied itself for—

I let out a scream as he took his cock

away. Did he not see how I throbbed and needed it?

It was David's turn again, and as he poked me with that long shaft of his, he didn't piston me like Auric and Tristan. On the contrary, he took his time, slowly pushing in, grinding, then retreating. Over and over and over.

It was enough to make me scream as he brought me to the edge of my orgasm and stopped.

"I think it's time," Auric announced as he lay on the bed beside me. "Teivel, place her on my cock."

Was there anything more decadent than one lover obeying another? Teivel's cool hands lifted me and positioned me over Auric's throbbing cock. When I would have shoved myself down, his hands stopped me, slowed my descent so that I was practically sobbing by the time I'd fully sheathed him.

A shudder went through me and another. I needed to move so badly, to rock upon that cock. But they wouldn't let me.

"Bend forward, Muriel." This time, I

was the one being ordered.

I threw myself on Auric's chest, loving how it allowed me to squirm on his cock.

He caught my lips and the sounds I made as the hard tip of a shaft probed at my rosette. Slick with my honey, the cock popped in, and I heard a sucked-in breath.

"It's so tight." Tristan couldn't hide his straining wonder.

"Push in farther," David advised. "She can handle it. Muriel likes it hard."

Did I ever.

As Tristan pushed his way into me, Auric thickened in my pussy. The man might have occasional jealousy issues, but he was a sexual creature at heart. He loved the decadence of sex. The musky aroma of it tickled the senses. The salty sweat slickened our skin. The pheromones perfumed the air and accompanied the gasps, groans, pants, and the fleshy smacks of skin on skin.

Tristan might have hesitated at first, but that didn't last. He was soon pounding at my ass, his fingers digging into my waist.

I felt the pleasure coil in him, his

balls tightening as they pushed against me, his cock pulsing until it exploded, and I drank not just his pleasure but magic in.

"Fuck me," he gasped as he came. And came, the hot jet of his cum making me even more slippery.

"David's turn," Auric ordered.

Tristan collapsed on the bed beside us, and David took his spot. As he pounded my willing flesh, I could feel my own pleasure rising. But I held on. I wanted a big one, a giant, screaming O.

"Suck on Teivel's cock." The words emerged through gritted teeth as I felt Auric straining to hold on as my pussy fisted him tight. I didn't have to look for my vampire's dick because he grabbed me by the hair and fed it to me.

The cool, smooth length of him gagged me, and I did my best to suck, even though I was mightily distracted by the pounding cadence of the cocks in my pussy and ass.

As cream hit the back of my throat, my ass, and my channel, more of it splashed my back, but I didn't really notice because my climax rocked me.

Rocked me like a fucking hurricane and burned me like a volcano erupting and drowned me under a sea of pleasure.

I couldn't scream, not just because of the shaft in my mouth, but because I had no air, no thought, nothing but bliss. And power.

So much power flooding into me.

The magic pooled in me, thick and pulsing, and my previous limits expanded to accommodate the new flavor I'd found. I glowed with it. I basked. I wanted to stretch my arms and sing with the glory of it. But this magic had a purpose.

I pushed the energy from me, shaping it like an invisible torpedo. I targeted it for one person—my dad. It arrowed through the wall, and I kept a link to it, watching with ghostly eyes as it zeroed in on my father, sitting in a chair, wearing a robe with his legs crossed—not exposing his junk for once. He read a book. Dear abyss, he read Heaven's *Dummy Guide to Being a Saint*.

The missile plunged right into my dad's chest. He never saw it coming, and his eyes widened as the magic I'd somehow fine-tuned to wipe spells exploded. It was the most powerful thing I'd cast and I had no idea how I crafted it, but it worked.

Layers of enchantment, some of them old, peeled from my father. Spells I never knew he wore. Were they his doing or someone else's? Didn't matter, they disintegrated before my magical blast.

To my surprise, my father grew larger, muscled. His face lost some lines. His hair grew dark. He turned into a veritable Adonis as my magic removed the spells covering him.

I'd wonder another day why my dad felt a need to hide his true visage. Why not take advantage of his good looks? Surely he had a reason, but that wasn't what I cared about.

Was my daddy still broken? I couldn't tell.

As the magic I'd projected dissipated, my otherworldly vision wavered before winking out. But with the amount of power I'd projected, surely I'd fixed him.

Except now I needed a fix, seeing as how I was empty again.

"Oh, boys." I tapped them on the

shoulders where they lay collapsed around me. "Anyone *up* for round two?"

Lucky me, they were. Even more awesome, Tristan decided that perhaps being a part of my family wasn't a bad thing after all.

As Lucifer's daughter, I might never enjoy a traditional happy ever after, but by all that was hellacious, I'd live life with adventure, zest, impatience, and lust. Oh, and chocolate, because contrary to what some folks say, it's better than bacon.

EPILOGUE

The arguing at my door woke me the next day.

"I'm waking her up," snapped my mother.

"We should give her some privacy instead of barging in," my father said in a soothing tone.

I sat bolt upright in bed.

"It didn't work," I exclaimed.

"What didn't work?" Auric muttered. "I thought we worked fine, all three times."

"I meant the spell on my dad. I thought it was gone, but listen." I put my fingers on my lips and stuck a boob in David's mouth when he opened it.

We held still and spied.

"Shall we go taste some wedding cakes today, my love?"

My mother made a noise of distress. "No, I don't want to taste cakes. I want you to tell me that they'll all taste like sawdust because I'm taking away your freedom."

"How could you think that? I cherish our upcoming nuptials. I've even written vows."

"Oh, Luc." My mother sobbed. I kind of joined her. My daddy was still broken, and I couldn't fix him.

Yet.

The giant orgy hadn't fixed my dad. The other sex marathons I had afterward hadn't either. Short of a lobotomy, I doubted much could. My daddy was, for all intents and purposes, a law-abiding yuppie. In our grief over his condition, my mother and I bonded.

Given the original Lord of Sin was somewhat incapacitated, as his heir in training, I got delegated to run Hell. In other words, I drew the short straw, and those who'd lost to me ran before I could demand we pull again.

Cowards.

How hard could it be to run Hell?

Twelve hours later, I was sobbing in a puddle of blood strewn with limbs, saying, "We have to get my daddy back. We have to."

Hell wasn't the same without his implacable iron fist. The damned souls were running amok. The minions weren't respecting me. And the demons were all fighting.

Lopping off a few heads helped. Stretching a few on the rack also played its part in settling some of the civil unrest. Throwing a few of the more annoying damned ones into the abyss for recycling? Yeah, that really calmed shit down. But I knew it was only a matter of time, minutes probably, before they started again.

We needed my daddy, the Devil, back. Like yesterday.

I screamed that in his face as a matter of fact as I shook him, wearing that bloody gray cardigan of his that he'd matched with respectable, pressed black corduroys.

"Where are you, Daddy?"

"Right here, Muriel." He beamed at me. "My beautiful daughter. Did you see the lovely gown I chose for you to wear for the wedding?"

Indeed I had, a fluffy, orange and yellow, cheerful monstrosity with flat-bottomed ballerina shoes so I wouldn't hurt my feet. All that concern about my feet, but what about my eyes?

What about the sanity of everyone in Hell? Because while my father might have lost his evil edge, he'd found something to occupy that space—wedding planning.

Lucifer was planning the wedding from hell. He even insisted on having bells.

Kill me now.

No wait. We had to kill Ursula. This was all her fault. And she'd pay for it with her life—once I escaped the dress shop Daddy dragged me to for my fitting.

Stayed tuned for Lucifer's story, Hell's Bells.

The End

AUTHOR BIO

Hello and thank you so much for reading  my story. I hope I kept you well entertained. As you might have noticed, I enjoy blending humor in to my romance. If you like my style then I have many other wicked stories that might intrigue you. Skip ahead for a sneak peek, or pay me a visit at http://www.EveLanglais.com   This Canadian author and mom of three would love to hear from you so be sure to connect with me.

Facebook: http://bit.ly/faceevel
Twitter: @evelanglais
Goodreads: http://bit.ly/evelgood
Amazon: http://bit.ly/evelamz
Newsletter: http://evelanglais.com/newrelease

Printed in Great Britain
by Amazon